# NASTY
# BOYS

# NASTY BOYS
## ROUGH TRADE EROTICA

EDITED BY
SHANE ALLISON

CLEiS
PRESS

Published in the United States by Cleis Press, Inc., 2246 Sixth Street, Berkeley, California 94710.

Printed in the United States.
Cover design: Scott Idleman/Blink
Cover photograph: Geber86/Getty Images
Text design: Frank Wiedemann

First Edition.
10 9 8 7 6 5 4 3 2 1

Trade paper ISBN: 978-1-57344-966-3
E-book ISBN: 9781-57344-985-4

# Contents

# INTRODUCTION:
# HE LOOKS LIKE
# TROUBLE

I can't stop thinking about you gripping me around the throat. You know just the right amount of pressure to apply as you take me from behind, thrusting, fucking me hard. You know just how much I can take, don't you, baby? I love the tough types, the rough men that have trouble written all over them. The first time I laid eyes on you with your tatted-up skin, scarred fingers and bruised knuckles, I knew that you were just the man I was looking for. You were a flesh-and-bone cliché parked outside of this crummy watering hole I frequented when I wanted to unwind. You were draped from head to toenail in leather and attitude. It was right then that I wanted you all over me; that I realized I would do anything. I purposely ignored you. You asked me if I had a light for the cigarette that hung from your voluptuous lips. Even though I don't smoke, I carry a lighter for men like you. The types of men my PFLAG mom warned me about. Hot shocks of ecstasy ran through me when your hand grazed mine as I lit your fag. *Is this really happening?* I thought. You told me not to go inside, that the drinks sucked and that you knew of a place that had better booze. You asked me if I wanted to take a ride with you on your motorcycle. I was scared, but I wanted you, so I obliged. I didn't know you. You were a stranger to me; you could have done anything to me, but I didn't give a shit.

I squeezed your helmet onto my head and saddled behind you on your bike. You told me to hold on tight. I wrapped my arms around your midsection. I could feel your muscles under the cotton of your T-shirt. The faint scent of gasoline and motor oil that was coming off of you made my dick hard. We weaved through traffic. I didn't notice how fast we were going. I just wanted to hold you.

We made it—not to a bar but your place instead. My stomach was filled with butterflies over you. I followed you inside your apartment that was surprisingly immaculate. You told me to make myself comfortable as you went to the bathroom to take a piss. The sound of your pee pelting the toilet water turned me on even more. Fuck, I'm such a masochist. We shared a bottle of vodka. I could taste your lips on my lips as I took swigs. It wasn't long before I was shit-faced drunk. We started making out soon after that, you forcing your tongue down my mouth like the rebel you were. As you pulled off my shirt and peeled off my jeans, you must have thought what an easy piece of ass I was. You ravaged me that night, taking full control. The next morning I woke up spent and sore, covered in leather and cum. It is to you that I dedicate this anthology, my love.

The best writing from the likes of Rob Rosen, Dominic Santi, Logan Zachary and Landon Dixon graces these pages. In addition, newcomers such as P. L. Ripley, Wes Hartley, Salome Wilde and Charlie Purcell have answered the call to capture what it means to be bad, to proudly veer off the straight and narrow into a world of punks, dirty cops, bikers, thugs and other ruffians.

I hope that you will enjoy reading these stories as much as I did. Now go out in search of your own trouble boy.

Shane Allison
Tallahassee, FL

# PERSIAN JOINT VENTURES

## Wes Hartley

When I scored this construction job as an apprentice rebar-stringer here in North Vancouver I didn't have a clue what I was getting myself into. I'd moved across the inlet from the Big City three months earlier. I found this okay ground-floor bachelor in a rundown apartment block in a blue-collar neighborhood where a lot of North Shore hard hats live. I've always had a thing for a certain kind of edgy blue-collar working boy with his rowdy bad attitude and redneck macho. This particular neighborhood is a perfect fit.

I've always been into dangerous blue-collar boys. What I like most about blue-collar boys is they're personal, they're obsessed with sex, they party like there's no tomorrow and if they're not closet cases or homophobes, macho blue-collar working boys will definitely let you suck it. Or make you suck it if you're lucky.

Blue-collar bad boys mean trouble. They're dangerous. They play rough. If you're looking to party-out and get personal with dangerous redneck boys, get used to a lot of hard knocks, broken promises and big surprises. Some of the biggest surprises are serious big surprises.

This company I'm working for is Persian Joint Ventures. It's an Iranian company. North Vancouver is celebrated for its populous community of transplanted Iranians. Back in the seventies when the shah got the boot and the wacko ayatollahs started power tripping, there was a secular exodus. More than twenty thousand freewheeling Persian escapees ended up in North Vancouver. All of the hardhats in the Joint Ventures crew are macho Iranian immigrants and first-generation Persian-Canadians. Most of them are in their early twenties. They're all hyper-masculine and rowdy and killer good-looking. To a starry-eyed queer guy like me, with my particular kinks and hard-wired preferences, the job site is dangerous territory.

The reason I'm feeling all these danger signals is I've just had a two-month-long, one-sided, major thing with this macho North Shore Persian bad boy. Khatan. Khatan came on like a bulldozer when he caught me eyeballing his Persian perfections one afternoon down on the Esplanade. Khatan has this infallible radar. When he caught me looking, he moved right in on me and started chatting me up like I'm some kind of pushover. Khatan was all decked out in these show-everything bike tights. He was looking to entrap starry-eyed pushovers like me. Khatan got me addicted to his Persian boner. Whenever he wanted head he'd give me a buzz, and I'd take care of it for him.

I quickly learned a lot about blue-collar Persian boys and how they see us pushover bottom boys. When a Persian boy finds out you're into him, he's all over you. He figures you want what he's got plenty of. So with my new job description and the crew of hypermasculine Iranian boys I'm surrounded by all day, you can get an inkling of what I mean when I say the Persian

Joint Ventures job site is a definite danger zone. It's like I'm seriously looking for trouble.

My first two weeks on the job are filled with the usual heavy-handed razz-the-rookie routines that are always to be expected. The foreman Sadiq is the exception. Sadiq treats me way differently than he treats the other seventeen hard hats. He always barks his orders at the Iranians in Farsi, but when he speaks to me in English he lowers his voice and talks way more personal. And, he partners me with the veteran on the rebar-stringing gang, Naz, who's easygoing and very patient with me. Naz is a nice guy, but definitely not my type. But there are a dozen guys on the crew who totally are.

The hypermasculine foreman is number one of the dozen, and I keep thinking he knows he is. He's definitely got his eye on me. Sadiq stares. He looks right into me. He gives me goose bumps and makes me feel nervous and jumpy. I notice him eyeing my butt when I bend over to pick up a length of rebar. I'm thinking Sadiq's got pretty good radar. Khatan once told me *most* Persian guys have bombproof radar. But, at the job site I'm trying hard to stay under the Persian radar. I'm feeling like it's not working.

It's Friday payday at the end of my third week on the job. So far so good. At noon when the lunch buckets come out I'm sitting with Naz and his good-looking nephew Farhan, wolfing down my lunch. I happen to look up high toward the office portable above us and I notice someone talking to Sadiq in Farsi. It's Khatan. He's smiling in my direction and eyeballing me while he's talking to the foreman.

I get this sinking feeling in my stomach and this strange tingling down between my legs. I get all sweaty and everything starts getting all "Twilight Zone." I feel like my Stealth Bomber has suddenly made this big noisy blip on the Persian radar.

After maybe five minutes Khatan ambles down the flight of stairs to the sidewalk and struts off. Sadiq turns around and leans over the railing and looks down at me and grins this killer ear-to-ear grin. He winks at me. Khatan has blown my cover for sure. Boys gossip. They never keep secrets. I don't know exactly what got said, or how Khatan happens to know Sadiq, but I know he ratted me out. Now Sadiq knows everything. I'm a total fuck'n mess for the rest of the day.

At five o'clock, the end of the shift, Naz's nephew Farhan comes to tell me the foreman wants to see me at his panel van. Sadiq parks his van against the wall of the old brick warehouse down the alley kitty-corner from our hole in the ground. Farhan delivers the message and clambers up the ladder to street level. At the end of every workday the Persian boys explode out of the chute like racehorses. On payday they vanish even faster.

I climb up the ladder and head down the alley toward Sadiq's panel van. His van is parked with the sliding door on the passenger side next to the wall. The side door is open and Sadiq is inside sitting on a big toolbox waiting for me.

Sadiq comes on strong right away. Things are different now. Khatan the Whistle-Blower took care of that. Sadiq smiles his all-knowing smile and reaches out and roves the palm of his hand all over my butt. The foreman reads my mind. He can tell I like him a lot. He wants to hear all about it. He wants to hear me say yes. *Yes* is his favorite word.

"You're queer for Persian penis, right?"

"Yes."

"You like me a lot, right?"

"Yes."

When I say yes to Sadiq my butt gets all sweaty and my dick gets totally stiff. I'm in serious trouble. Sadiq can tell he's got me sweating. His aggressive come-on is making me want to say yes.

"You wanna be my yes boy, right?"

"Yes."

"You wanna see what I got for you, right?"

"Yes."

Sadiq is referring to what he's got for me in the bulging crotch of his rumpled black coveralls. He unzips the long zipper and bares his full frontal all the way down to his what-he's-got-for-me. His outstanding what-he's-got-for-me is good-looking like he is. It's kinda big and it's pointing right at me.

"You like my big penis, right, Yes boy?"

"Yeah, a lot."

"You want it, right?"

"Yeah, a lot."

Sadiq's strong hand grips the back of my neck and steers my head down to his crotch.

"Give your new Persian boss a nice big kiss."

I kiss my new Persian boss.

"Kiss him again."

My favorite Persian words are *yes* and *boss* and *kiss him again*.

First thing Saturday morning I get this inaugural call on my new cell phone. Yesterday afternoon when he dropped me off at my place, Sadiq gave me one of those prepaid throwaway cell phones. For his calls only. Sadiq wants me to know he's coming by to pick me up at ten o'clock tonight. He tells me he's got a big Saturday night surprise for me. He puts me through my yes boy paces and starts getting personal. His porn talk gets me rock hard and makes me feel nervous and jumpy. I get all sweaty and I can barely breathe. I get goose bumps all over.

"You miss my big penis, right?"

"Yeah."

"You like it a lot, right?"

"Yeah."

"You can still taste it, right?"

"Yeah."

"You want it right now, right?"

"Yeah."

I'm encouraged to agree completely with Sadiq's rhetorical Q&A. The foreman gets his yes boy to say yes to anything he wants. It's easy to see that my interrogator expects a lot of appreciation. He wants to hear me appreciate his penis. Sadiq's power word for his dick is penis. This has got to be how victims of the Stockholm Syndrome must feel. I'm identifying with the ultimatum of my intriguing captor. I've morphed into his queer yes boy. I'm in deep trouble now. Sadiq's got me wanting what he wants me to want.

My dick is seriously hard all day long in anticipation. I feel like putty. I'm weak in the knees. I feel anxious and vulnerable. I feel hopelessly queer for Sadiq. I *can* still taste Sadiq. The gym-locker aroma of his sweaty crotch got way up my nose. When he detonated he ordered me to swallow. He didn't have to. I always swallow when it's perfect.

At ten o'clock my new cell phone rings. Sadiq is three blocks away. He doesn't like to be kept waiting. I'm at the curb in front of the apartment when the black panel van pulls up. Sadiq is glad to see me. I can tell because his masculine signifier is vertical, jutting up out of the open fly of his jeans. I climb into the shotgun seat beside him and slam the door. I lean across in the dark and acknowledge his prerogative with a kiss. Sadiq gets what he expects. I bend down and kiss it again.

Sadiq guns the engine and we careen up the street burning rubber. Sadiq doesn't say anything, he just smiles knowingly. I don't say anything either. He reaches around over the seat and retrieves this large empty gym bag from the back of the van. He drops it on the seat between us. "Get your clothes off, now. Put everything in the bag. I want you naked."

I take my clothes off while Sadiq watches. I stuff everything into the bag and zip it closed. Sadiq tosses the bag into the back of the van. I'm naked. As ordered. Sadiq can tell I'm liking this a lot. My hard little stiffy is ratting me out. I'm feeling anxious and sweaty. I feel totally vulnerable.

Sadiq pulls up in front of the big swinging gate at the Persian Joint Ventures maintenance yard. The industrial-zone street is dark and empty. No people and no traffic. An orange streetlight illuminates the entrance to the supply yard with a ruddy glow. Sadiq hands over a ring of keys with one singled out and tells me to get out and unlock the gate and swing it open. I barefoot-it out of the van and unlock the big brass padlock and unfasten the heavy chain. The sharp gravel is harsh on the sensitive soles of my bare feet. I swing the gate inward and Sadiq drives in. I swing the gate closed and loop the chain around the gatepost.

Sadiq parks in the far corner across the dark lot, his front bumper butted up against the tall board fence. He parks alongside a huge, current-model, luxury RV. One of the Joint Ventures partners owns the big RV. He's given the foreman carte blanche to utilize the motel-on-wheels for his afterhours whatever. I barefoot-it over the harsh gravel to where Sadiq is waiting for me. He unlocks the door with the key and steers me like a sleep-walker up the steps into the palatial camper van.

The sprawling, name-brand RV is gilt-edge plush and loaded with all the extras. The floor is paved with expensive Persian carpets. My attentive host steers me toward the rear end of the bus roving his hands all over my naked butt as he steers. In the master bedroom at the back of the bus, Sadiq turns me around and kisses me assertively. A deep, lingering masculine kiss. He darts his tongue into my mouth and wrestles my tongue into submission. Sadiq's kisses taste like red licorice. He roves his rough hands all over my butt while he kisses me aggressively. Sadiq makes me feel sexually naked and totally vulnerable.

My Persian Prince lowers me onto the king-size bed, lights candles in holders on the side table. In the light of the candles I finally see Mr. Perfect perfectly naked. He stands between my spread legs and lets me have a nice long look at what he's got for me.

Sadiq is tall and lanky. His physique is thoroughbred marathoner. Lean muscularity, tapering torso, narrow waist, nice long thighs, and melon buttcheeks. His muscular penis is clean-cut and good-looking like he is. It looks to be an eight-incher.

The foreman's Persian profile is total desert sheik. His stylish jet-black curls surround his head like a halo. He's got a mocha-latte complexion, dark mahogany eyes, a straight nose, full lips, a chin dimple and a teaser smile. His smile says, "I know you want it," and his steady gaze calls all my bluffs.

Sadiq is midtwenties. He's maybe three or four years older than me. The bloom of adolescence still brightens his masculine good looks and adds spice to his confident bravado. Naz's nephew Farhan told me Sadiq is a nephew of one of the Persian Joint Ventures' owners. That explains the reason a young guy like him is foreman of such a big project.

Sadiq picks up this little bottle from the side table and unscrews the cap. The label says Oil of Almonds. He pours a puddle of oil in his left hand and slathers it all over his penis and balls. He grabs my ankles and lifts my legs high over my head exposing my main attraction. He pushes two fingers into me and rotates them, working them deeper and oiling up my rear entry. He pulls me forward to the edge of the bed and plants the slick head of his troublemaker against the oily pucker of my socket. He starts applying pressure. He doesn't force it in, he just keeps applying steady pressure. Sadiq wants in. He's waiting for me to open up and welcome him in. My rosebud opens and pulls him all the way in.

Sadiq impales me. He grinds his crotch against my stretched-out socket and makes me squirm. He takes total charge and power-fucks my tight squeeze bareback. He probes and intrudes and pushes my limits to the max. His pummeling is relentless. He likes to crank his persuader all the way out and then slam it back in all the way. Sadiq fucks me ragged. His jackhammer onslaught rocks and rolls the motel-on-wheels and rattles the dishes in the kitchenette. Sadiq zeroes in on my sweet spot. His power surge overloads my capacitance and blows my circuit breakers. My reciprocator capitulates and I gush jets of sticky stuff all up my stomach and chest.

Sadiq is very pleased with the progress of his yes boy. Now he knows I want what he wants me to want. Now he's got visual proof. He smiles and smears the sticky proof of his expertise all over my chest with the palm of his hand. He found my sweet spot. Now he knows how to make me squirm.

Sadiq unplugs. He grabs my legs and flips me over and piles on top of me. He reconnects his plug-in and lets me know he's barely scratched the surface. He puts in an extra-long shift and goes for some major overtime. He punches my time clock five times on the night shift, unloads three times, and stays marathon hard. His muscular third degree leaves a very strong impression.

Monday morning I show up for work at Joint Ventures' hole in the ground. Everything is totally different now. I can still feel Saturday night's big surprise. I'm still feeling anxious and edgy and on high alert. Sadiq is everywhere like always, but he's keeping a low profile.

At noon the foreman's cell phone goes off in my pocket. He's told me to keep it on me 24/7. I'm expected to take his call whenever he buzzes me day or night. When I hear Sadiq's voice my susceptible bone jumps to attention, and I start sweating.

Sadiq tells me he's at the office window at street level overhead looking down at me. He's got me in his sights. He wants to know am I hard? I tell him, yeah. Am I thinking about his penis? Can I still feel it? Am I eager for another all-nighter? Yeah, three times. Especially the can-I-still-feel-it. He wants to know, did I take care of that detailing issue he called my attention to? Yeah, I did. He wants to have a look-see. He's expecting me up at the office at quitting time.

At five o'clock the job site is evacuated in a flash, and I'm compelled up the ladder to the street. I mount the stairs up to the catwalk. The door of the office portable is open. I step inside and the foreman motions me to close the door behind me. "Show me the new detailing."

To show him my new detailing I have to take off my work shirt and drop my pants. I take off my flannel shirt and drop my pants to my ankles. I lift up my T-shirt over my face so he can check out my new detailing. My styling new Middle Eastern detailing gets his full approval. Last night I shaved off all my body hair from my neck down. My sleek bare-naked crotch makes me look like a grade-school boy. My little naked stiffy looks even littler now.

"Turn around, I wanna see the pretty butt." I turn around and showcase my pretty butt.

Sadiq likes what he sees. He tells me I look perfect now. He says I'm not his little yes boy anymore. I'm his pleaser now. He straddles the corner of the office desk and spreads his legs. He unzips the fly of his rumpled work-khakis and reefs out his tireless Persian pleaser.

After the Monday daily grind and after-work workout in the office portable, I make it back to my apartment overwhelmed by my Persian obsession, marked with his masculine essence, and completely made over to suit his stiff requirements. Sadiq's taste and the tang of his sweat, his approving smile and the sound of his voice, my shaved crotch and raging hard on, my appropriated and occupied butt, and my 24/7 cell phone and new job description earmark me as the boss's queer pleaser. I'm on edge and on alert. I'm anxious and fidgety. I'm under pressure and under surveillance and on notice. Whenever his cell phone rings my dick jumps to attention. I'm Sadiq's pleaser now. I'm eager to please him. This is the way it's gonna be.

I could use a megadose of fresh perspective. My worked-over libido is seriously over-the-top. My Persian fixation has compromised my queer mobility. I've been ambushed by my own hard-wired preferences. My libido needs a serious makeover. I need to realign my out-of-whack queer continuity. I need fresh input. It ain't gonna happen.

Wednesday afternoon I'm on my way home from work when the cell phone goes off in my pants pocket. My dick rears up on cue, and I feel the ringing way up my butt. Sadiq wants a rematch tomorrow night at his RV-incognito. He's expecting me at exactly ten o'clock sharp. He's got another big surprise for me. He's giving me lots of notice. He's wanting to watch his bottom boy squirm.

Thursday all day long all I can think about is Sadiq's big surprise. Whenever he catches my eye he grins or winks or grabs his crotch the way certain rappers do. He's keeping me off balance and anxious. He's watching me squirm. Persian machos like to keep their fuck boys eager and squirming.

At exactly ten o'clock I park my rust bucket pickup truck on the dark street near the gate at the maintenance yard. The gate chain is hanging loose and I see Sadiq's van parked next to the motel-on-wheels. There's a faint ruddy glow behind the curtain

in the side window in the back of the RV. I let myself in, close
the gate behind me and crunch across the gravel to the sugar
shack. I take my clothes off and enter the party zone in the rear
of the bus. Sadiq is sweaty-naked and ready to rock. His big
surprise is too.

The foreman's big surprise is his former brother-in-law
Pasha. Pasha is the crane operator at the job site. He's in his cab
up above us all day so I haven't seen much of him during the
past month. Pasha is definitely the hottest-looking young guy in
the crew. Sadiq's got great taste in ex-brothers-in-law.

Pasha is extremely good-looking. He's short and stocky, and
his humpy physique is well-upholstered all over. He's dark and
masculine and squeaky clean. He's twenty-four, five years older
than me. A Persian bachelor. Short curly black hair, bedroom
eyes and kissy lips. He's got a wide gap between his front teeth
and a grin like a chipmunk. Extra-big hands. Short legs, massive
thighs, a great big butt and a muscle-bound dick. Pasha's dick
looks like it works out a lot at the gym. It's a real beauty same
as he is. It's cut. All Persian boys are cut. Pasha's big beauty
is looking to get up-close-and-personal right away. I drop to
my knees between the massive thighs of Joint Ventures' crane
operator. Pasha steers his heavy equipment into my mouth and
grinds his crotch into my face. His crotch smells like the gym
lockers up in heaven and his big beauty tastes like birthday
cake.

Pasha batters the back of my throat with his choker while
Sadiq cheers him on. Then Sadiq massages my tonsils too.
Sadiq changes my oil and Pasha's persuader puts some serious
mileage on my Persian persuader-squeezer. My reciprocator is
seriously persuaded. Pasha revs his big engine and makes me
gush big time. Former-Brother-In-Law's enthusiastic incursion
is riveting. He keeps pounding it up me for ten minutes after he

detonates. After Sadiq's jackhammer follow-up, Pasha goes for second helpings.

Late Friday afternoon I run into Sadiq and Pasha on Upper Lonsdale a few blocks from the job site. They're heading to a shish-kebab eatery and they've got Pasha's eighteen-year-old brother Rustam with them. Rustam's got a job for the summer as rookie helper at Joint Ventures' supply yard. Rustam is a younger version of his humpy big brother. He looks like trouble. Rustam rocks my casbah. He gives me the eye and turns on the Persian boy charm. Pasha says something to Sadiq in Farsi and Sadiq laughs and so does Rustam. Pasha and Sadiq volley Persian one-liners back-and forth for the benefit of Little Brother. Sadiq winks and lets me in on the joke. The joke's on me. My butt is the butt of the joke.

Maybe ten minutes after our close encounter Sadiq's cell goes off in my pocket. My dick jumps to attention on cue and my butt tingles. Sadiq tells me his pleaser's got a new admirer. Rustam likes what he sees. He's been asking a lot of questions. He's looking for answers. Sadiq tells me he gave rookie Little Brother the cell phone number. Rustam's gonna be giving me a buzz right away. Sadiq says he knows I'm gonna love Rustam.

Rustam gives me a buzz right away and keeps me buzzing. That's what rowdy blue-collar boys do best.

# BAD BOYS
# GET SPANKED

## Rob Rosen

I'd seen him around the neighborhood, hanging out on the corner, at the liquor store, on a curb or two, always with a cigarette dangling from his mouth. Lord only knew what he did for a living, if anything. Still, I knew to avoid him, cross the street if it was dark, when it was just him and me out there. Hedge my bets some.

Then again, from the comfort of my apartment, I could stare all I liked.

Naked from the waist down, that is.

Binoculars zoomed the fuck on in.

I'd start on his face: slender jaw, stubble on top of stubble, crooked nose, eyes the color of the sky on a hot August day, blue squared; hair slicked back, dark as coal. Made you want to cream right there, only that's not when I usually did it. Nope, I inched the binoculars down a bit as I stroked slowly away, stopping on the V-necked T-shirt, at the mess of hair poking up and out, black and curly, probably coarse, I figured. Imagined. Dreamt.

"Nice," I'd groan, binoculars moving farther on down, the T-shirt tight, jeans even tighter. "Mmm," I inevitably added, picking up the pace on my cock as I landed on his crotch, at the bulge dead-center.

Except, that's not what made me shoot.

Close, but no cigar.

A few more inches down is what did it. The hole in his jeans, at the knee, ripped wide and low; part of the thigh revealed, part of the shin, acres of flesh that filled up the lenses. Like I was in on a little secret. A swatch of skin meant just for me. Hair and muscle framed in frayed denim. Mine all mine.

Then *WHAM!* I'd shoot, legs buckling, back arched, sweat flinging off of me as the come spewed up and out and down, splattering on the floor below in giant gobs of aromatic white.

I'd set the binoculars down next, sigh, and go back to my life, forgetting about him until the next time. Then the time after that. Thanking the dudes at Minolta for their technology and extra-strong zoom lenses.

I might've been okay with just that, too, had it not been for a late-night need for a bite to eat and an empty fridge on my part. I ducked out to the corner store for a loaf of bread, some mayo, some sandwich meat and a bag of chips.

I almost made it out of the store and back across the street that night. Except almost is not quite good enough. Especially when I dropped the bag, the mayo jar flinging out before rolling down the sidewalk and around the corner, stopping smack-dab against his hip.

I turned said corner and froze. There he was, sitting on the curb, staring up at me. His blue eyes were sparkling like sapphires beneath the lamppost light, leather jacket over the usual T-shirt, ripped jeans tantalizingly close, the flesh like a beacon in the cold, dark, night.

"Sorry," I squeaked out, suddenly bolted to the spot. "Can I, um, can I have my mayo back, please?"

He wiped his hands on his jeans, pocketed his cigarette, grinned as he hopped up and held the jar out to me. "Fuck off," he spat, quickly yanking it away, the grin replaced by a sneer. Still sexy, but that's not what I was thinking of at the moment. More like, *Could I outrun him if need be?* And *Please don't let there be a need be.*

"Come on," I said, voice shaky. "Just give it back, please."

"I found it," he said, closing the gap between us, closest I'd ever been to him.

"I dropped it," I countered with, readying myself for a pummeling.

"Shit's bad for you," he replied, eyeing the content label.

"Shit makes a sandwich taste better though," I told him, forcing a smile on my face that belied what was going on behind the veneer. Like terror.

"Cool," he said, stepping around me and shoving me as he went by.

I stood there staring at him as he went from sidewalk to street. "Where you going?" I asked.

He paused and hollered over his shoulder, "Your place. For a sandwich. Like I said, cool."

My heart galloped through a furlong. *My place?* "You, uh, you don't know where I live, though."

He stopped and turned, midstreet, not a car or person in sight. Like a standoff at the Not-So-Okay Corral. "You live in the building across the street," he replied, the sneer again evident. "Seen you go in. Seen you go out."

*Fuck, he knows where I live.* "Keep the mayo. We're good."

He sighed and returned my way, stopping an inch in front of me as he pushed me in the chest. "We're good"—push—"when

I say we're good"—push.

I gulped and wiped off the sweat that had trickled down my face. "Hope you, uh, hope you like ham."

He grabbed the bag from my hands and started back across the street again. "My fucking favorite."

I watched him walk toward my building, jeans hugging that fine, tight ass of his, and I weighed my options. Which appeared to be nil. Mainly because he knew where I lived and could just as easily torment me at a later date. Still, to be on the safe side, if there still even was one of those, I texted my work email to let myself know who the killer was, hoping someone would find it at a later time, post-funeral.

Then the gulp was repeated as I followed him across.

"Name's Roger," I managed, in step with him now.

"Goodie for you," he snapped, swinging the bag in front of him, not even bothering to look my way.

We reached the front door of my building. He stopped. I stopped. As did my heart. I unlocked the door. "After you," I told him.

He shoved past me. Which made him lose his footing. Which made him fall. Which made him go *splat* inside my entryway, his body instantly prone, limp.

I quickly hopped over him, pulled him forward and closed the door behind us. Suffice it to say, he was out cold, and I was royally screwed. *Leave him here and call an ambulance?* I thought. *What if he comes to and starts robbing all my neighbors? Or worse.*

I sighed, crouched down and picked him up. Thankfully, he wasn't all that heavy, dead weight though he was. Not so thankfully, I lived three flights up. And no elevators. Still, in for a penny, in for pound, I figured. Meaning, up I trudged, hoping beyond hope that no one would exit their apartment and catch me. Because this was something I simply could not explain away, like a trick or a date.

And this was clearly no date.

In any case, minutes later, and with me drenched in sweat, we were inside my apartment with him on the floor, breathing nicely, the lump on his head already apparent, but at least no blood. Then I went for the phone to call the ambulance. Then I stopped when I realized that he was going to be awfully pissed at me, even though it was his fault for tripping. Fucking Murphy's Law.

I stared down at him, his legs splayed, the tear in his jeans revealing hair and sinew and creamy white flesh, at his head thrown back, slack jawed, eyes shut tight, the blue kept at bay. Peaceful and serene. However temporary it would be.

So I did the only thing I could think of and I found some rope, put my Boy Scout training to some good use, finally, seeing as I never really had a need to start a fire or build a lean-to in the heart of the city. Then I tied him to my pullout sofa, both hands, all before I headed back to the phone to call for the ambulance.

Only... "What the fuck?" I quickly heard above the drone of the dial tone.

I dropped the phone and rushed over to him. "You okay?"

He glared up at me, anger in those pools of blue that made them boil over, steam rising. "Fuckin' let me go, asshole."

I was breathing heavy now, more out of fear than because his shirt lifted and the love trail revealed itself, a six-pack with a seemingly extra set of cans a second later as he twisted and turned and failed to move the sofa an inch. "You tripped. I carried you all the way up here. And now I'm going to call an ambulance."

He, too, was breathing heavy, his eyes in a squint. "Fuck if you are! How am I going to pay for a doctor?"

"City General," I replied.

He snickered. "Might as well call the morgue then." Then he locked eyes with me. "For you and me both if you don't let me go." Then he started hollering a string of obscenities that made the walls rattle.

I fell to my knees next to him. "Please stop screaming!" But he wouldn't. So I slapped his face. And then he did. Temporarily. So I slapped him again and then punched him in the chest. And that indeed did get his attention. That and a soft moan from between his bee-stung lips. Again I punched him, and again he moaned. Only this time it was joined by a tenting in his jeans.

Go figure, a hoodlum who dug pain, tied to my pullout sofa in the middle of the night, that damned Murphy's Law run amok.

I closed the gap between us, my face up to his face. "What's your name?"

He spat at me, the saliva trickling down my chin. I walloped him again, slapped his belly, his rock-hard cock swaying in those ripped jeans of his. "Troy," he grunted, the rage replaced by something more telltale.

I stared down the length of him, the hole at the knee split even more. I reached in and up and back. Dude was going commando. I grabbed his balls and gave them a sharp tug. "Behave, Troy."

He winced and arched his back. "So dead, dude."

I pulled again, harder this time. "Says the man tied to my sofa with his balls in my grip." Then I leaned down and returned the spit in kind, another slap administered to his chest. "Now, I said behave."

He quieted down, no longer squirming, just huffing and puffing. "Let me go," he rasped, eyes again locked onto mine, so much blue you just about wanted to take a dip in them. *Please.*

I released his balls and moved my hand up an inch, grabbing on to his shaft, his moan replaced by a groan. My hand continued up, up, up, counting the inches off in my head, stopping at a steely hard seven. "The please was nice, Troy," I made note, pulling my hand down his pant leg and out the hole. "But it doesn't quite suit you."

He glared up at me, not a blink. "Yeah, what does then, *Roger*?"

I grinned and reached for his T-shirt, which I hiked up, belly and chest revealed, the hair curly, soft as down as it turned out, nipples jutting out like eraser tips. "I'll let you know," I replied, twisting and turning each of them as he again writhed on the floor. I leaned in closer, our faces now flush. "You like that, Troy?" I whispered. "Like your nipples tugged?"

His eyelids fluttered as I yanked and pulled on them some more. "Fuck you, Roger."

I slapped at his crotch, which was still rock-solid rigid. "You wish." And if there was a genie lurking about somewhere, I hoped he was listening to that wish.

In any case, I ran my hands through his thick chest matting, caressing and yanking at the hairs as I went along, his sighs repeatedly replaced by grunts, the loudest as I popped open his jeans, his bush revealed, thick and ebony, curly, shaft exposed, jeans just barely keeping the beast in check. "Let me go," he repeated, rather lackluster-like this time as he watched my progress.

"Why should I, Troy?" I asked, crab-walking to his feet, to remove his sneakers and ratty socks. Big feet, too, hairy toes, beautiful arch, which I slapped and tickled, until he kicked and squirmed again. Meaning, he got another series of chest slaps until he simmered down some, panting even harder now. I reached up and held my hand menacingly above his chest. "You gonna behave now?"

"Fuck you," he said again, and the hand came crashing down. The sneer returned, but, for now, he was keeping quiet.

I finished where I'd left off, my hands inside his waistband, the denim yanked down in fits and starts, cock at last springing free, the hole no longer needed to see that tantalizing skin and hair as I pulled the jeans off entirely, his prick ramrod stiff and pointing up at me, thick and leaking, the wide, helmeted head glistening in the light above us.

Again he grunted as I pushed his legs apart and sat in between them, slapping the shaft and sending it springing, left, then right, his moaning like a swarm of bees in my ears. His cock turned beet red before I spat on it and gave it a slow, even stroke.

"Mmm," he hummed, head tilted back, chest rapidly rising and falling.

"Mmm, indeed," I moaned back, unzipping my jeans to free my prick, which I slapped on his balls as he yelped and squirmed some more. Then I reached for his calves on either side of me, lifted up his legs and put them on my shoulders. I stared down. Cock and balls and asshole. The holy trinity. "Mmm," I repeated, mouth watering at the sight.

He lifted up his head, eyes again locked with mine. "Make me come, dude."

I grinned and slapped his ass instead. Hard. Harder. Hardest. "Bad boys get spanked," I told him. "Then, maybe, they can come. If they ask nicely."

Up my hand went, then down, the red again rising, pushing through the dense matting of hair that fairly blanketed his stellar ass, his moans louder with each progressive slap and spank and smack, with each whack and wallop, my cock so thick it felt like it could blow at any minute.

"Please," he now pled, a tear streaming down his cheek as the last thwack was administered. "Please make me come, Roger."

It was about as nice as he was gonna get, though it still didn't suit him all that well. Plus I was ready, too. And then some.

So, with my left hand, I grabbed onto his pole of a prick, my right moving up and down on my own thick shaft, a spit on his dick, a spit on mine. In sync I pumped, my eyes again on his, his on mine, laser-locked, both of us panting up a storm.

He shot first, his body trembling from stem to stern as his head twisted from side to side, a moan rumbling through his body and into mine, a thick band of spunk flying up before landing on his belly. It was followed by another and yet another, three white gobs that joined as one and then dripped over and down onto my carpet.

Needless to say, the sight of it, the smell of it, was enough to send me into orbit. On my knees I went, then aimed, shot and fired. Every nerve ending in my body was suddenly on fire as my cock spewed and spewed and spewed some more, drenching his tummy yet again as my groan outgunned his moan, until the very floor beneath us seemed to shake.

Gasping for air, I stared down at the heavenly mess. "Now *that* suits you, Troy."

"Fucker," he spat. "Now untie me."

*So much for the please.* Still, I did have to untie him. Which didn't sit all that well with me, needless to say.

I pushed my prick back inside my jeans and inched over to his face. "Fine," I relented, voice nearly catching in my throat. "But no funny business."

He didn't reply, just stared up, watching as I reached for the rope. Good Boy Scout that I am, it only took me a minute or so to untie him.

And, of course, then there was that aforementioned funny business.

Only, I wasn't laughing.

As soon as he was free, he jumped, taking the wind out of me as his body landed on mine, my hands quickly above my head as he held them in place. His face moved in, inches from my own, the sea of blue quickly obliterating everything else. He panted down at me, me up at him. I watched, waited for the inevitable, steadied myself for the pain.

I winced as he opened his mouth. Except, rather than spitting or biting or reeling off a string of obscenities, he gave a smile so wide as to put the man on the moon to shame. "You owe me a ham sandwich, Roger," he said. "With mayo."

"Fuck you, Troy," I replied, craning my neck up so that I could bite his lower lip.

He pulled away and hopped back up, dick still dripping as he turned and headed for the kitchen. "After the sandwich, Roger," he told me. "After the sandwich."

I pushed myself up on my elbows, my eyes landing on the binoculars by the window, the jeans crumpled on the floor, and the hole I knew so well, and I whispered, "Maybe during, dude. Maybe during."

# CALL-BOY
# KILLER

## Logan Zachary

His nude form slipped out from beneath the sheets. Sweat ran down his tan, firm torso. His body hair was shaved off, except for a neatly trimmed triangle above his semierect cock. His balls dangled low between his legs as he made his way to the shower. His tight bubble butt defied gravity with each step. The fleshy muscles rippled beneath the smooth pale skin.

"Are you going to join me?" he asked over his shoulder. "It won't cost extra."

The man sat up in bed and rested his back against the headboard. "Warm it up for me," he said in a low growl.

His twenty-three-year-old chiseled body was in the gym every day to stay firm and tight for his clients. He demanded top dollar, and he received it. Stepping into the shower, he turned the dial to hot. The water felt good as it pelted his sore muscles.

This guy had made him sweat. He never had to work this hard to earn his pay, but this man was different. He closed his eyes and tipped his head back, enjoying the cleansing spray.

He felt a presence behind his body in the stall before the calloused hand caressed his butt. A thick finger slid into his crease and explored downward, deep, to his opening. The tip sought entry as it pressed against the tight sphincter muscle.

The man slipped his finger out and brought it to his mouth. He sucked on it, lubricating it with his own spit, and replaced it, readying the hole for entry.

With one quick motion, he slid his digit in and up to the first joint. He made a circling motion. The finger continued inward as the boy pressed back and down upon it. The water and spit made the entry easy. His digit disappeared to the knuckle and waited. Slowly, it withdrew, and two fingers entered.

"Ahhh," the boy moaned. The hot water ran down his face, across his chest and down to his rising flesh.

The man shifted his weight behind him; his heavy cock ran its head along his smooth leg and explored the cleft between the two perfectly formed orbs. The fingers slid out, and the fat mushroom head replaced them.

The boy felt the pressure and took a deep breath as the man drove himself inside, to the hilt. The thick shaft plowed the tight muscle open. The boy arched his back, accommodating the cock in its entirety. He felt two hairy balls slap between his legs. He could feel the prickly warmth of the man's hairy body, as it crackled against his soft flesh.

"Take it slow and easy. I want to make this last," the boy said.

The man wrapped his arm around the boy's neck and pulled his head back as he thrust inside again, deeper this time.

The boy felt a warm tearing of soft tissue, but continued his play. He would get a big tip for this one, despite a little bit of blood and pain. He could feel a warm thick fluid slide down the inside of his leg and mix with the running water. Hopefully, the boy thought, this guy would come quickly, and he could get out of there.

The man grabbed him by the hair and pulled his head back. "Say it." He drove his cock in again harder than before. "Say it."

"Ouch!" the boy said, trying to pull away from the man.

The man's legs wrapped alongside the boy and held his backside so he could plunge in again. He thrust his throbbing member deep inside.

"I need a break," the boy said, turning his head, "and a condom…"

But the man's hand pulled the boy's hair and controlled his head.

The boy felt his arm being released as he heard the sound of the shower curtain being pulled back. It resounded in the small area. His body relaxed, maybe the man was almost done.

A cool breeze entered the shower and swept around their bodies as the steam escaped from the stall. Goose bumps rose across the boy's wet body. He was just starting to enjoy the rhythm when a new sensation jolted his body. White heat slammed into his back. The sudden blow took his breath away.

As the boy moved from under the shower nozzle to get more air, a red bubble erupted from his mouth. The boy spat out a warm, salty taste and saw red swirl down the drain. *Blood?* he thought, and then the pain registered. A wet sucking sound came from his back as he inhaled. At first, he thought the man had withdrawn from him, but another blow struck his back a little lower this time.

A wet cough erupted from the boy, as the white heat retracted. He turned his head to see what was happening, when a flash of silver swung around his chest and rose to his throat. A quick slash across his neck, and a new, warmer and thicker wave descended down his chest. His head tipped forward, as the room grew foggy. He didn't understand the dizziness that was making his legs grow weak.

Another thrust in his bottom drove him forward. He used the momentum to propel his body away from the man. He felt the thick mushroom head pull out of his tender opening. It sounded like a cork from a champagne bottle. His feet slipped on the wet shower floor, as he saw the metal blade flash again.

The boy wondered why he was on his back. How had he ended up here?

The man slipped his erect flesh down between the boy's slender legs and plunged it inside the boy. The blade entered his chest at the same time.

The world turned a dark red. With each thrust and blow that filled the boy's world, he felt like he was swirling down the drain. Despite the hot scalding water, his body felt cold, but the pain was easing. His body relaxed. His head flopped back and his eyes stared at the ceiling, unable to see what was happening to his perfect body.

The knock on the door jolted Randy out of his thoughts. He pressed the RECORD button on the tape player and carefully closed the drawer on the bedside dresser. He left the drawer open slightly so the small microphone could record what happened inside the room. A video camera would have been better, but the problem was where to hide it. And besides, it was too late now.

A thin layer of sweat broke out across his brow. He pulled back the bedcovers and turned off the lights above the bed. He walked to the door and looked at himself in the mirror. Randy's blond hair was cut short and neatly combed. As his hand touched the doorknob, he glanced back at the bedside dresser. He hoped that he had left the drawer open wide enough to record, but not too far, so that this guy wouldn't be able to tell that it was open.

Before opening the door, he pressed his eye to the peephole. A man with wavy black hair stood outside. Several buttons were open on his red shirt, revealing a hairy chest. His jeans were tight and hugged his body.

Was he the one? Randy's mouth went dry, and his heart pounded in his chest. He wiped his clammy hands on his pants and opened the door.

"Hi," the man said in a low voice.

"Hi," Randy said in a higher pitch than he had wanted. He swallowed hard and lowered his tone. "Come on in." He stepped back and held the door open.

The man bowed slightly and entered. He walked past the foot of the bed and turned around. "Sorry, I'm late. Traffic was backed up. There must have been an accident."

"No problem," Randy said. His eyes darted to the dresser drawer and then back to the man.

The man glanced over to where Randy had looked. His eyes searched the bed and the dresser, before returning his gaze to him. "What do you like to do? Did you have any ideas for tonight?" His dark eyes bore into Randy.

"I was lonely and just wanted a little company." Randy worried his hands as he spoke.

"And I have a few bills to pay." The man extended his hand and rubbed his thumb against his middle and index fingers.

"Oh! Yeah, that's right. Do you want the money up front? Or after…?" Randy looked into the man's eyes. He could feel a stirring in his groin. Despite his anxiety, he was starting to get turned on. Damn, this guy was sexy. What a shame.

"Whatever you prefer. The customer is always right." His dark eyes held their stare.

"Maybe we should get comfortable." Randy motioned to the bed with his hand and stopped. *And let's just rush right into this,* he thought.

The man ran his hand through his hair, pulling the waves away from his face and letting them bounce back into place. His hands went to the cuffs of his shirt and unbuttoned them. He started to work the ones down the center of his chest and paused. "This is what you meant, right?"

"Sure. Let's see the goods." Randy closed his eyes. He couldn't believe he had just said that. His eyes shot open and he smiled. "I mean, maybe if we sat down and got to know each other first."

More of the man's hairy chest was exposed. A thick dark mat covered his toned torso evenly. His skin appeared a dark olive in complexion, suggesting an Italian heritage or hours of sun exposure.

Randy sat on the side of the bed and waited for the man to join him. He wet his lips as he approached. He could almost feel this guy's body heat radiating from him the closer he came.

"My name is Chase," he said simply.

"I'm Randy."

Chase's hands reached across Randy's chest and started opening his buttons. His fingers skillfully worked down to his pants. As the last button popped free, Randy's body tensed.

Chase paused for a second before pulling the shirt open, exposing a smooth, tan chest. His skin was a rich bronze showcasing the lean chiseled body beneath.

Randy could feel his arousal grow hard and painful in its tight confinement. He wanted to adjust himself, but wasn't able to move with Chase's current position.

Chase pulled the shirttails free of his pants and used the fabric to move Randy closer to him. He extended his neck and brought his mouth over Randy's. His lips captured Randy's full lips and pulled them into his mouth. The taste of man and mint entered and passed between the men. Tongues explored and vied for position. Chase pulled Randy's lower lip into his mouth and rolled it between his teeth. He released him and waited.

Randy pressed forward. His lips sought Chase's. Forgetting the tape player, he moaned as he drew Chase's tongue into his mouth. They removed each other's shirts, which were discarded on the floor.

Chase's hands caressed Randy's body and pulled his smooth chest against his hairy one.

Randy lay back on the bed, and Chase rolled on top of him. Both men kicked their shoes off as their pelvises rubbed against each other.

Randy's hand worked down Chase's back and slipped beneath his waistband. He continued downward, his fingers digging into the tight gluteal muscles that flexed and pulsated under his touch.

Chase reached down and unbuttoned his jeans, giving free access to Randy.

Randy could feel the furry covering of Chase's backside. He squeezed and kneaded the mounds of meat. As he caressed, he worked the jeans and briefs down, lower.

Chase's hand found Randy's pants and unbuttoned the waist and slowly drew the zipper down.

As his fly opened, the pressure that had been building slowly released. Randy could feel his erection swell with the extra room, and it grew to its full length. A wet spot had soaked through his underwear.

Chase's hand passed over it as he pulled the pants lower.

Both men wiggled out of their pants, which were kicked

onto the floor. Free from their constraints, they pulled the cover sheet back and slipped underneath. Neither man remembered removing his socks. Clad only in their briefs, the men rolled on top of each other, their hips gyrating in circles, rubbing their erections against each other.

Chase's fingers found Randy's waistband and slipped underneath. He worked them down over his butt, exposing his backside under the sheet.

Randy's hands pulled Chase's briefs down in the front and freed his erection.

Feeling his freedom, Chase removed Randy's underwear the rest of the way. Both pair of briefs flew over the side of the bed.

Chase was on top of Randy and lowered his 180 pounds down. His chest and body hair tickled Randy down the entire length of his body.

Randy spread his legs, opening his pelvis for Chase's. He could feel the low-hanging balls dangle between his legs and against his own. He rocked his hips in time with Chase's, feeling a thick cock slide along his own shaft. Precum mixed on Randy's abdomen as their mouths kissed deeply. Tongues and teeth pulled on their lips, back and forth with an intensity that neither man had felt before.

Chase lowered his body slightly on the bed, and his erection slipped down between Randy's legs and probed a tender spot.

Randy raised his legs, exposing his butt for easier access. He pulled one hand back from Chase's hairy chest. His other one continued to comb through the jungle as his free hand worked up, behind his head, and under a pillow. His hand found what he was looking for and started to emerge.

Despite the stealthy movements, Chase noticed when Randy's hand slipped away. As Randy's hand started to come out from under the pillow, Chase captured his wrist. Chase's legs pressed forward and his body dove onto Randy, trying to pin him to the bed.

Randy was taken by surprise, but reacted instantly. He tucked his body into a ball and rolled as Chase dove. Both men sailed over the side of the bed and landed on the floor. Naked limbs struggled to free themselves from the attack and the sheets. Hands fought to block and hold the other man down.

Chase was stronger and had the advantage of being on top, but Randy's lithe body almost slipped free. Chase recaptured the hand Randy had pulled out from under the pillow and held it to the floor. He pounded it until Randy's fingers opened, and a silver-wrapped condom flipped out.

As suddenly as he started the attack, he stopped it.

Randy felt him stop and held still. He turned his head to see what had happened.

Chase broke the silence. "Was that what you were reaching for?" He pointed to the condom.

Randy looked over. "Yes."

"Okay, then. I'm going to let go of you." He released Randy's arm and pushed himself up into a sitting position.

As Randy sat up, he realized that he was buck-naked with a raging hard-on. He reached over and pulled the sheet to cover himself. "I thought you had to say that you were a cop if you were working undercover?"

Chase pulled the sheet off of the bed, exposing Randy in the process.

Randy quickly pulled the blanket from the bed and wrapped it around his waist.

"I'm not a cop, but what about you?" Chase demanded, as he reached for his pants. His huge cock stood straight out proudly.

"I'm an investigating reporter." Randy said, trying to regain his dignity. His cock throbbed under the blanket.

"So where is your byline?" Chase asked.

"Well, I'm working on that. I need to finish investigating this case before I can get my byline." Randy nodded his head to punctuate his point. "I'm looking for the Call-Boy Killer."

"You're just a reporter; maybe you should let the PIs do their job." Chase buttoned his bulging pants and pulled on his shirt.

"You're a…"

He slipped on his shoes and walked to the door. "I'm Chase Knightly, PI," he said as he opened the hotel room door.

"And I know what PI stands for, pain in the—"

But the door slammed shut, cutting off Randy's last word.

The next day, Randy walked down a dark corridor and glanced at the piece of paper in his hand again. "It should be around here somewhere." He rounded the corner. A door with a frosted-glass window read: CHASE KNIGHTLY, PRIVATE INVESTIGATIONS. He shoved the piece of paper into his pocket and knocked on the door. It looked like something out of one of those black-and-white noir movies.

No answer.

Randy rapped again and when there was no answer, he tried the doorknob. It turned in his hand, and he entered. The door opened into a waiting area with a large desk and another room behind it. No wonder he hadn't heard the knock.

"Chase?" he called.

A shadow approached the inner door and opened it. "Can I…?" Chase's voice trailed off, as he saw him. "Oh, it's you."

"Well, it's wonderful to see you again too." Randy tossed Chase's underwear on the desk. "You forgot these yesterday."

"How did you find me?" Chase asked.

"I let my fingers do the walking." Randy demonstrated with his hand.

"The phonebook." A light shown in Chase's eyes.

"Good detective. I see why you deserve that painted door."

"Okay, what do you want?" Chase demanded, cocking his hips and resting his hands on them.

"I came for a job." Randy ran his finger over the typewriter on the desk.

"I need a secretary, I don't need a...a..." but Chase didn't finish his thought.

"We're working on the same case. We should team up and solve it together."

Chase said nothing.

"I'll do anything you want." A sly smile played across Randy's lips.

"Do you know how to type?" he asked.

"I can use a typewriter," Randy ran his fingers through his hair, "and more, but most offices have computers."

Chase nodded his head, but didn't look convinced.

"My friend, Kyle, was killed by this guy. I want to find out who did it. Besides, you need me." Randy cocked his head and rested his hands on his hips, copying Chase's stance.

"I've been doing just fine, all by myself," Chase said.

"Yeah, like last night." Randy rolled his eyes.

But before Chase could say anything, Randy continued. "The killer likes..."

"Yes," Chase leaned forward.

"This"—Randy ran his hands down the side of his body— "not that." He motioned toward Chase.

"What are you talking about?"

"If you had done your research, you'd know that all of the victims have been smooth, blond, young guys. Not dark, hairy, old...older men."

"I'm not..." Chase began, then he paused for a second. "So,

you want to work as bait?" Chase asked.

"I'll work undercover. Not under the covers like last night, but I'll help with the investigation. I'm willing to do whatever needs to be done to find Kyle's killer."

Chase brought his hand to his chin and rubbed it. His eyes narrowed on Randy. Finally, he said, "I'll hire you if you accept working under a few conditions."

Randy bit his lower lip. "And what are these conditions?"

"You won't put yourself in danger. You need to follow my orders to the letter. I don't allow any mavericks around here."

"You'll be the only one," Randy mumbled under his breath.

"What was that?"

"That was number one." He smiled at Chase.

Chase didn't look convinced, but he continued. "You'll help out around here during the day. Answering the phone, taking messages, typing reports and such." He walked back into his office and reached across his desk, flashing his tightly covered butt in the process.

Randy rolled his eyes. "Anything else?"

He returned with a stack of files. "No, but you can start right now. File these." He slammed them down on the desk. "You're hired," he said, and grabbed his underwear and went back into his office.


Randy struggled to the side of the bed, hanging on to his jeans with all of his might. The bald man lay across the bed, totally naked. Randy noticed that his butt was as smooth as the top of his head. "I think that you may have misunderstood..."

"I bought you for the night, so I get you for the night. Now, get those jeans off so we can get started." His fingers dug into Randy's waistband and pocket, as the sound of denim ripping echoed in the hotel room.

The rip in his favorite jeans startled him, allowing the man's nails to dig into his flesh and draw blood. "Ouch! That hurt!" Randy pulled back with all of his might and fell onto the floor.

The naked man's hands released. Once he saw Randy sprawled on the carpet, he pounced, knocking Randy's head against the wall.

Stars spun around as the room swayed from side to side. The world started to turn dark, when the door burst open.

"Get off of him now!" Chase stood in the doorway. His frame seemed to fill the opening from their position on the floor.

The naked man screamed as Chase reached for him over the bed. He rolled off Randy and crawled around the bed and out the door.

Chase watched as his pale, smooth backside flashed him and disappeared into the night. He turned back to Randy. "Are you okay?"

Randy rubbed the back of his head and willed the world to stop moving. Chase had two heads, then one and then back to two.

"Are you okay? Was he the one? Do I need to..." He pointed out the door.

Randy shook his head and stopped. "He thought I was backing out of the...deal, which I was, but he wouldn't listen to me about us working undercover."

"So you don't think he was the killer?"

"He was desperate, for sex, but not murder. He wouldn't take no as an answer."

Chase looked down at Randy's side and saw the nail marks. "Wow that must hurt." He tenderly touched the bright pink skin, which jumped underneath. Gently, he gathered him up in his arms and placed him on the bed.

"He ripped my favorite jeans."

"And it looks like he did a number on your skin."

"He was our last suspect. The last one in Kyle's book... ouch."

Chase reached over and unbuttoned Randy's jeans. "Let me take a look at that scratch."

Randy's body tensed. "I don't have any underwear on."

"It's not like I haven't seen what you have."

"What!"

"I mean that you don't have anything different than any other guy, so..." Chase flushed as he worked the zipper lower, exposing a mat of thick brown hair. He pulled down one side and examined the wound. "It isn't too deep, but it's going to hurt for a while. No blood, but a dark red sore."

Randy lay back as a pain shot up his back. "Ow," he moaned, and he rolled onto his side.

"What's wrong? Did you hurt your back? Let me see." Chase pulled Randy's jeans down, exposing his upper leg and buttocks. His deep tan lines revealed the Speedo he wore when he enjoyed the sun. Chase slipped the pants off his legs and rolled him over. A pink mark covered his bottom, along with a spot on his back. His hands reached over and massaged them tenderly.

He could feel Randy's body relax under his touch. He started on his back, but worked lower to the bubble butt. His fingers kneaded the firm ass.

Randy moaned.

Lightening his pressure, he asked, "Am I hurting you?"

"Anything but."

Chase could feel a stirring in his pants. His fingers explored down into his crease and cupped both smooth, white cheeks. His large hands could palm each orb perfectly. His thumbs found a tender spot and circled it.

Randy pulled his head back in pleasure. He could feel his erection oozing from Chase's touch.

"Is it getting hot in here?" Chase looked at the open door and down at Randy's exposed backside. He walked to the door and closed it. He stood looking down at Randy's nude form. Before he knew what he was doing, he had stripped off his clothes and joined him on the bed. His erection rubbed up and down Randy's tanned, hairy legs as he returned to his massage.

Randy humped the bed, and the sheets caressed his aroused skin in time with Chase's hands. He pushed back as thumbs pressed down on his opening.

Chase licked his thumbs and returned to work massaging him.

Randy could feel the slickness between his cheeks and relaxed his sphincter muscle further.

Chase moved higher on his back, and his thick erection slid along the crease. The precum lubricated its path. He reached across the bed and pulled out a condom. Tearing the package open with his teeth, he slipped the sheath on his cock. He spit on his hand and lubed up the rubber. His dick sought out the tight opening, as Chase reached around in search of Randy's erection. His spit-covered hand mixed with precum and slid easily over the hard member.

Both men's pelvises rocked in time, as Chase slowly entered Randy. His hand tightened its grasp as the pace intensified. He thrust himself deep inside and pulled back, his hand following the rhythm.

Randy's body welcomed the entry and matched pace with Chase's. He drove his cock into Chase's hand with each thrust inside his butt. "Faster. Harder," he breathed.

Chase did. He plunged in faster, harder. His hand pumped on Randy's cock, faster, harder. Sweat coated their bodies, adding to the movement. The attack on Randy and their investigations were forgotten. The release of the intense pressure that was building between them was their only goal. Waves of pleasure stimulated their nerve endings as their need grew. Chase moved closer to Randy, his hairy chest pressed against his back as his hips drilled into him.

Randy bucked back, meeting Chase. The tip of his cock slipped through Chase's fingers as a clear fluid continued to seep out. The tingling pulsated with his heartbeat. He could feel Chase filling him from behind. His prostate throbbed with excitement.

Then a wave hit him that couldn't be stopped. It started in Chase's balls, rode along his dick and burst forth. As the thick cream hit Randy's gland, it continued through his body and down along the shaft of his erection. He came in Chase's hand, his pleasure exploding between his fingers. Each throb spread through both of their bodies. Wave upon wave of need rippled into a warmth that covered both men.

They lay spent on the bed, breathing heavily as their hearts slowly returned to a normal rate. Chase rolled away from Randy, pulling out of him with another wave of ecstasy. Sleep descended on them.

"Chase Knightly Investigations. They do the crime, they serve the time. Detective Randy speaking."

Chase walked to the door and scowled at him.

Randy smiled and nodded his head. "Yes... Yes... Naturally... He will... Trust me... Okay then... Bye."

Chase stood at the door and waited. "Well?" he asked.

"Well what?" Randy spun around in his swivel chair.

"Who was that, and what did they want?" Chase resisted the urge to tap his foot on the floor.

"Oh, that?" He pointed to the phone. "Wrong number."

Chase could feel his face begin to burn. "What did I say about...?"

"All right. All right. I ordered lunch." Randy held up his hands in surrender. "Get out the lightbulbs and the rubber hoses."

The door to the waiting room opened as Randy was on his tirade. Chase held up his hand to stop him when he recognized Officer Morgan Pierce. "Pierce, it's great that you could stop by." He extended his hand.

Pierce walked over and took it. After his greeting, he looked at Randy. "When did Chase hire you?"

Randy flushed. "He didn't hire me, I'm..."

And Chase's hand clamped over his mouth. "Not even a week ago. I needed someone to type and answer the phones."

Randy's teeth nipped Chase's palm, and he pulled it away. "I'm Randy. Nice to meet you." He stood and took Officer Pierce's hand and smiled. Randy's eyes roamed over his even white teeth and deep brown eyes. His black hair was cut close to the scalp, and his blue uniform hugged his muscled body. A small tuff of black hair escaped from his collar hinting of a forest farther down.

"Don't let him push you around, Randy. He tends to become bossy when he's working on a case."

"Tell me about it." Randy rolled his eyes. "Are you working on Kyle's murder?"

"Kyle?" Pierce looked confused.

"I mean Jamie Pratt, only his closest friends called him Kyle," Randy said.

"We should go into my office and talk." Chase stepped around Randy's desk and ushered Pierce inside.

Randy stood with notebook in hand and made to follow.

"We won't need you in here," Chase said, closing the door tightly.

"We won't need you in here." Randy mocked Chase's tone, but he stood his ground. He leaned forward and cocked his neck to hear what was going on inside.

"...I think we are running out of leads..."

"...If we used his black book..."

"Why does that stupid door have to be so sound resistant?" Randy asked.

The intercom buzzed. "Randy? Hold all calls," Chase said. The intercom clicked dead.

"I should be in there helping. Hold all calls, ha, that's a laugh. I bet you'll be fawning all over Officer Pierce's blue eyes."

Randy walked over to the filing cabinet and strained to overhear their conversation. The words were still muffled. He placed his ear against the wall.

"I thought we had him last night, but..."

And then there was a knocking on the door.

Randy spun around. "Damn it, why did that delivery boy have to be so fast? Come in," he called, ear still pressed against the wall.

The intercom buzzed again. "Can you keep it down out there?"

"Great, they can hear everything I say out here, but I can't hear anything in there."

The delivery boy looked confused. "Are you talking to me?"

"No." Randy reached into his back pocket and pulled out his wallet. "How much do I owe?"

"Twenty-one fifty."

Randy pulled out two tens and a five. "Keep the change."

The brown wrapped package was set down on his desk, and the delivery boy took the money. He smiled, "Gee thanks." He tipped his baseball cap and left.

"I'll be running out for my own lunches from now on." He

sat down at his desk, as an idea popped into his mind. What if he turned the intercom button on in Chase's office when he brought in his lunch? An evil smile played across his lips.

Just as he pulled out Chase's lunch, the inner office door opened. "Thanks for stopping by Pierce. I'll be in touch."

Officer Pierce nodded at Randy as he left.

"Darn it all," Randy said, under his breath.

"What was that?" Chase asked.

"Don't it beat all? He is such a good-looking cop."

Chase smiled and said nothing.

"Lunch is served. Did you want it out here or in there?"

"I'll take it in there. I have a report to finish and a few calls to make." Chase picked up his food, closed the door and sat down at his desk.

Randy swallowed hard. Was Chase uncomfortable about what happened last night? He glanced into the office through the frosted window. Suddenly, he wasn't so hungry.

Later that afternoon, a handsome man entered the office. He looked around the room for a place to sit. Randy was on the phone and motioned to the chair in front of his desk. He nodded his head as he listened to the caller going on and on about something that he already had lost interest in.

Randy slid a clipboard toward the man and mouthed, "Fill it out."

The man's dark eyes bore into Randy's, making him swallow hard from their intensity. He pulled out a gold pen from his jacket pocket and started writing.

"Yes...yes...I see...aha ..." Randy's head bobbed with every word.

Chase's head popped out of his office. "Mr. Stevens? You're here."

Randy stopped talking. "The Mr. Stevens who owned the motel?"

Chase and Stevens said, "Yes," at the same time.

"I'll call you right back," Randy said, and hung up the phone without a clue as to whom he had been speaking with.

Chase ushered Stevens into his office, and Randy followed him with his notebook. Chase didn't see him slip in behind his desk and set his notebook down. As he turned he saw him. "That'll be all, Randy," he said.

"But ..." Randy started.

"I'll call you if I need you. I think I can handle it from here." Chase gently pushed him out the door.

But before he could close the door, Randy pushed past him, and reached over the desk. He pressed the intercom button down with one hand as he picked up his notebook and lunch wrappings with the other. "I need this, and I'll get this out of your way," he waved it under Chase's nose as he passed. "Besides, I have other things to do..."

And the door was shut in his face.

Randy resisted sticking out his tongue, knowing the frosted glass wasn't thick enough to mask his expression. He raced back to his desk and inserted his earpiece and settled down in his chair.

The phone started to ring, but he ignored it.

"As you know, we're trying to solve this case as quickly as we can. I'm sure you want your business to..." Chase paused, searching for the right word, "...return to normal."

Randy smiled to himself. "If that's what you call it."

"I really don't know what I can tell you that I haven't already told the police. I don't work Thursday nights, so I wasn't even there. I doubt that..."

Randy sat straight up. Thursday night! He opened the bottom

drawer of his desk and pulled the folders of the three victims. Tim Masters was murdered two days before Valentine's Day, February 12th, and that was a Thursday. He opened the next file. Ronald Durrett died March 25th, a Thursday! And Randy knew that Kyle had been killed on a Thursday night, since they had plans for the weekend that never happened.

He pushed the earpiece farther into his ear.

"Jamie Pratt was a nice kid. It's sad to see such a waste of a life so young, so full of possibilities," Chase said.

"The streets are rough out there, especially when you're in that line of work," Stevens said.

"I'm sorry to have wasted your time," Chase said. "I just thought that you may have seen something or heard something that could help."

Randy heard the chair scrape across the wooden floor, and he heard footsteps near the inner office door. He pulled his earpiece out and shoved it into his desk. The door opened up and he sat erect in the chair.

Chase held the door open and waited for the man to exit. He shook his hand as they walked out. "Thanks again for coming down here. You saved me a trip."

"I was in the neighborhood anyway, so it was no problem." Stevens's eyes met Randy's and held there for a few seconds.

Randy stood up and walked around the desk. He extended his hand to him. Stevens's cold stare held as he reached out for Randy. He smiled, but it didn't warm his stare. "Sorry, I couldn't help you find out who killed Kyle."

Chase stopped and stared. He looked at Randy with a questioning look in his eyes.

And then Randy knew. Only those who knew Kyle used his real name. He grasped Stevens's wrist and pulled it down and back. He tried to bring it behind Stevens, but he wasn't fast enough.

Stevens spun on his feet and rounded behind Randy. He grasped him around the neck.

Before Chase could respond, Stevens reached inside of his jacket and pulled out a gun and held it to the side of Randy's head.

Chase held his hands up and stepped back.

"Don't anyone move!" Stevens warned, as he stepped back, pulling Randy with him. "I'll pull the trigger. You know I will."

"But why?" Randy asked.

"They made me do it. They all did. Tempting me like that— strutting by with all of their johns and tricks, and never once giving me a second look." He pressed the gun harder into the side of Randy's head.

"But you're a married man," Randy said with disgust in his voice.

Stevens shoved Randy away from him.

Randy's body slammed into his desk and knocked the wind out of him. His hands hit the typewriter, which he grabbed hoping to stabilize himself. He and the typewriter slid across the top and off the end of the desk. He landed in a heap on the floor, but sprung to his feet still clutching the typewriter. As he swung around, Stevens raised his gun and aimed it at him. Randy swung his arms to the side and spun his whole body around, sidestepping slightly and bringing the heavy black metal machine down on Stevens's arm.

The weight of the typewriter struck with such force, the gun went off.

Randy turned to see where Chase was, and if he had been hit.

Stevens turned in time to see Chase dive for both of them. The momentum of the typewriter and the force of Randy had slammed Stevens down to his knees. Chase's impact took all three to the ground. As Stevens's arm hit the floor, the gun exploded in his hand again.

Randy's ears rang from the closeness.

Chase crawled over to join Randy. Both men rolled Stevens onto his stomach and made sure his gun was pointed away. Chase rose and slammed his foot down on Stevens's hand and secured his gun hand to the floor.

Randy grabbed his head as it rose from the floor and slammed it down. A sick crackling came from his nose, as a wet splat sounded. Stevens's body went limp.

Randy pushed away from him and looked down, ready for his next assault. It never came.

Stevens was out cold.

Randy turned to Chase. "Are you okay?"

Chase nodded as he kicked the gun out of reach.

"I want you to admit that you were wrong," Randy said sitting up on the floor.

"I was wrong? About what?" Chase asked. "Who killed Kyle?"

"No. That I knew how to use a typewriter," Randy smiled.

"All right, I guess you do." Chase bent over and picked it up and set it back on the desk. "Well, I guess that settles that." He extended his hand to help Randy up.

Randy frowned. "You mean my job is over? I'm fired?" His face fell.

"What? You want this job? I thought you were going to write the byline of a lifetime with this story. How will you move up in the ranks of journalism?"

"Well." He paused and took a deep breath. "I kind of got fired." Randy blushed. "I didn't get my copyediting done, and they didn't really know that I was working here undercover...so they fired me."

Chase stared at him.

"It was all of this extra work and time you made me spend here. I couldn't get anything done at the newspaper."

"So, it's my fault now?" Chase smiled.

"Yeah."

"So you'll be looking for a new job then?"

"I guess," Randy sounded disappointed as he stood and wiped himself off.

"Well, you can keep your job here, if you want, but on one condition."

"And what's that?" Randy asked.

"You'll have to learn how to use a typewriter and not like that." He pointed to the bent frame on the desk.

"Who uses a typewriter anymore anyway?" Randy complained.

"I just wanted to know that you were able to type, because I'm planning on getting a computer, and I don't want you using it to subdue our next criminal. Okay?"

"Whatever you say boss," Randy said, as he hugged Chase and held him close. "Is this okay?"

"Are you asking about what happened last night?"

"I just wanted to know where I stand."

Chase pressed Randy against the desk, forcing him to sit down. "I don't want you to stand." Chase reached down and picked up one of Randy's legs. He pulled a pair of handcuffs from his back pocket.

Randy's eyes widened.

"Don't get excited. These are for him on the floor, but if you're a good boy"—Chase leaned forward and kissed him—"we'll see."

# DICKED

## Michael Bracken

I was sitting at the hotel bar nursing my second Jack-and-Coke when a man straddled the empty stool to my left and unbuttoned his jacket. I examined his reflection in the mirror as he caught the bartender's attention and ordered a gimlet with a twist. He wore a navy-blue two-piece suit over a crisp white shirt, a rep tie still firmly knotted at the collar. Finger-length black hair lightly frosted with silver had been parted on the left with laser-like precision and a day's growth of beard shadowed his square jaw. His hands were free of jewelry but a gold Rolex peeked out from his left shirt cuff.

The bartender presented the man's gimlet and then faded away to attend to a portly gentleman in an ill-fitting brown suit sitting at the opposite end of the bar. Several stools remained empty between the portly gentleman and me, and my new companion could have settled onto any of them.

"Long day?" I asked without turning. I had blown off two other men before his arrival.

He eyed my reflection and then turned to face me. "Long enough," he said, but the way he said it let me know he wasn't talking about his day. "Yours?"

"The same."

He smiled. As he turned to face me, his jacket opened for a moment. I caught a glimpse of his shoulder holster and the .38 tucked into it, and I marveled at the skill of his tailor. If I hadn't known to look for his sidearm, I might never have suspected it was there because the cut of his jacket completely disguised its presence. I wondered which pocket held the leather wallet containing his badge and I.D.

As he rested his hand on my thigh, he said, "I haven't seen you here before."

"It's my first time," I said. "A friend suggested this place."

"Your friend's stayed here?"

"He said it was the best place in Dallas to meet like-minded men of discretion."

"It certainly is," my new companion said. He sipped from his gimlet. "Where are you from?"

"St. Louis," I lied. "I'm traveling on business."

He nodded at the ring on my left hand. "Married?"

I lied again, feeding him exactly the information he needed to hear. "Wife, two kids, house in the suburbs."

He finished his drink and caught the bartender's eye. "Another of these," he said as he touched his glass, "and another for my new friend."

My third Jack-and-Coke was as weak as the first two, an arrangement I'd made with the bartender when I'd placed my first order.

As my new friend and I sipped our drinks, his hand inched up my thigh to the bulge at my crotch, and we continued our small talk as if nothing unusual were happening. I continued feeding him the lies he needed to hear and, after he finished his second gimlet, I suggested we finish our conversation in my room.

His eyes narrowed as he examined me. For a moment I thought I'd been too forward and was afraid that I had aroused his suspicion, but he squeezed my thigh and said, "I think I'm up for that."

My suite on the top floor was part of the lie, implying a disposable income I didn't actually posses, and he was suitably impressed when I pushed the door open and turned on the light.

In the privacy of my suite he became less refined and less reserved. "Why don't you take off those clothes and show me what you've got?"

I matched his crudity. "I need to take a leak first."

"You do that."

While I was in the bathroom, he opened the minibar without asking and fixed himself a drink. He was finishing it when I returned wearing one of the complementary bathrobes I'd found hanging in the bedroom closet.

He'd used the time I was out of sight to remove his jacket and shoulder holster, and he'd neatly hidden his sidearm beneath his jacket when he'd draped it over the back of the couch, much as I'd hidden the wire I'd been wearing.

He grabbed hold of the sash keeping my robe closed and unthreaded it. The robe parted, revealing my nudity beneath. He must have liked what he saw because he pushed the robe off my shoulders and watched as it slithered down my arms and fell to the floor at my feet.

Then he grabbed my jaw in one meaty fist, tilted my head back and kissed me deep and hard.

"You came all the way to Dallas for this, didn't you?"

This time I didn't have to lie. "Yes," I said. "Yes, I did."

My friend had told me exactly what to expect from the cop who held my jaw, from the approach at the bar to the rough sex to the post-sex shakedown. What I didn't know is if he would give me the same name he'd given my friend. "You got a name?"

"Does it matter?"

"I need to call you something."

"Call me Dick," he said, with the same lack of originality he'd displayed seven months earlier.

"Okay, Dick," I said as I slipped one hand under his belt and into his boxers, answering my question even as I asked it. "You ready to do this?"

His thick cock throbbed in my hand as I wrapped my fist around it, and I felt a slick drop of precum tickle my wrist. I used my free hand to unbuckle his belt and unzip his slacks. As his pants dropped to the floor, he pushed my shoulders down until I knelt on the floor in front of him.

I peeled his boxers out of the way and took the head of his cock between my teeth. That wasn't enough for Dick and he pressed against the back of my head until I took his entire length into my oral cavity. The unkempt black nest of his pubic hair tickled my nostrils and made me want to sneeze.

Dick held my head between his hands as he drew his hips back and pushed forward, slamming his cockhead against the back of my throat and bouncing his heavy balls off my chin. While his cock was thick, it wasn't long enough to make me gag, and I easily accepted every one of his thrusts. I grabbed his asscheeks and held tight, digging my nails into the firm flesh and leaving tiny half-moon indentions as I scraped a bit of his skin under my fingernails.

His ball sac began to tighten and his hips began moving

faster, so I was prepared when Dick suddenly stopped and fired a thick wad of hot spunk against the back of my throat. I swallowed and swallowed again, and when his cock finally stopped spasming in my mouth, Dick released his grip on my head.

I pulled away and sat back on my heels. My cock stood erect, straining for attention I knew he wouldn't provide, so I wrapped my fist around it and jerked off while Dick undressed. A good-looking man, stocky without being fat, he was the type of guy I would have invited into my bed even under other circumstances. As it was, I was enjoying myself more than he could have ever imagined.

Dick had removed all of his clothes and placed them with his jacket before I came, and I shot a thin stream of cum across the carpet that almost reached the couch where he'd placed them. He saw what was happening and said, "Hey, watch the clothes. I have places to be later. I don't want to have to go home and change."

I still had my hand wrapped around my cock when Dick hooked a hand under my arm and pulled me to my feet. His cock had begun to regain its former stature.

"You got lube?"

"In the bedroom."

He propelled me in that direction, through the doorway toward the king-size bed. An unopened tube of lube lay on the nightstand and he grabbed it. He opened it, slathered some on his cock and then spun me around and pushed me facedown on the bed. He grabbed my hips and pulled upward until I realized what he was doing and drew my knees under me so that my ass stuck up in the air.

Dick slathered lube into the crack of my ass, massaged it into my asshole until he could slip one and then two fingers into me. He used far more lube than necessary and it dripped down the underside of my ball sac onto the bed. A moment later he withdrew his fingers and pressed his cockhead against my slick sphincter. He grabbed my hips and thrust forward, driving his cock deep into me.

Even though I'd been expecting it, I still wasn't quite prepared for how rough he was. His grip was so tight he bruised my hips as he drew back and slammed forward, his lube-slick cock sliding in and out of me faster and harder.

My cock grew hard as Dick fucked me, and I was so turned on I almost forgot why I was there. I reached between my thighs and caught some of the lube dripping from my ball sac. Then I wrapped my fist around my cock and pumped in counter-rhythm to Dick's ever-quickening thrusts.

He came first, with one last powerful thrust that almost drove me off my knees. I only remained as I was because of his powerful grip. As he fired hot spunk into me, I continued pumping my fist until I came, sending my own wad of spunk onto the bedspread beneath me.

Dick held me until his cock stopped spasming, and then he stepped back, releasing his grip on me as he pulled away. I collapsed on the bed, lying on my own wet spot, but I didn't care.

I rolled over and looked at him.

"Worth the trip?" he asked.

"So far," I said with a smile.

"You think you can do this again?" he asked with a smirk.

I knew one of us would get fucked again before he left, but I shook my head.

He stepped into the bathroom and left the door open while he urinated and washed his crotch. Then he walked into the other room and I watched through the open door as he dressed.

I knew just the question to ask when he lifted his jacket off the back of the couch and revealed his shoulder holster. "Why do you have a gun?"

He strapped on the holster, slipped on his jacket and returned to the bedroom. He retrieved a worn brown wallet from his hip pocket. He flipped it open to reveal his badge and ID. "Because I'm a cop."

"A cop?"

"And soliciting's a crime." He returned the wallet to his hip pocket.

I feigned befuddlement. "Soliciting?"

"You approached me in the bar, invited me to your room and offered sex for money."

"I did?"

"Be a shame if your wife got word of this." He stepped into the bathroom, found my clothes, and dug through my pants for my wallet. He opened it, thumbed out the driver's license, and added, "Doug."

I understood how he had been able to intimidate my friend. "But I didn't do what you said I did."

"A real shame, Doug," he continued. "What about your employer? Think they'd be interested in knowing what you do when they send you out of town?"

"I—I—" I stuttered. "What can I do to make this go away?"

"Are you offering to bribe me, Doug?"

"No, I—I just—"

He smiled. "A thousand dollars. This could all disappear for a thousand dollars."

"I—I don't have that much money with me."

Dick looked in my wallet. "I can see that." He thumbed out the cash, counted it, and said, "One-eighty-seven is a good start."

"But—"

"That's okay," he said as he pocketed the cash and thumbed out my debit card. "There's an ATM in the lobby."

"I have a two hundred a day limit."

He thumbed out my credit cards. "Cash advances on these'll make up the difference."

The time had come to turn the tables. "And if I don't pay you, you'll tell my wife and my employer?"

"I thought that was obvious."

"So you're shaking me down."

He shrugged. "Call it what you will."

I reached for the remote and switched on the television. An image of the two of us sitting at the bar downstairs filled the screen.

"I think I'd call it early retirement, *Dick*." I folded my hands behind my head. "You turn in your badge or copies of this tape get sent to Internal Affairs, the DA's office, and—"

His smirk disappeared. He interrupted me by reaching under his jacket and removing his .38. "You son-of-a—"

"I wouldn't if I were you." I pointed at the television. Seven months earlier Dick had shaken down my friend and now my friend sat in the next suite watching and recording everything as it happened. The scene on the television screen switched from the recording of Dick and me in the bar to a live feed of Dick pointing his .38 at me.

I watched my cock get hard and said, "It looks like you're getting fucked this time."

# ITCHY TRIGGER

## Dominic Santi

The dildo up my ass was almost as fat as Sir's cock. He'd squirted a tube of lube up my ass, stuck the huge silicone cock's suction-cup base onto a bar stool in the laundry room, and snarled, "Sit!" Then he stood there, his massive, tattooed arms folded over the thick mat of hair curling out around the edges of his tank top T-shirt. He watched impassively while I straddled my sore, naked body over the stool and balanced my feet on the lower rungs. I slowly and painfully lowered myself, stretching my well-slicked asshole down over that monster cock until my ass was planted firmly on the rounded leather cushion. I sat there, panting, my whipped ass throbbing and my asshole quivering over the huge fake dick. Sir took my cock and my balls in his palm and stroked my softened shaft between his thumb and fingers.

"It's time for some serious training, punk. Keep your hands on the stool and don't move."

I obediently gripped the seat, moaning as my cock stretched hard and horny into the strong, calloused heat of Sir's hand.

Even though I knew I was in for very unpleasant day, I loved it when his voice rumbled deep and mean in his chest.

"Your dick's getting hard fast, punk. Your untrained punk dick's getting hot and stiff like it's ready to shoot all the way from your balls." Sir leaned down and kissed me, thrusting his tongue into my mouth, reminding me again how much shorter and skinnier I was, and how much smaller my otherwise respectably sized dick was in comparison to his. I sucked his tongue voraciously, tasting last night's whiskey and the sesame seeds from his morning bagel. My cock jutted up against my belly as his hand slid around me. His thumb pressed in firm, hard circles into the V just below my dickhead.

"Tell me when you're going to shoot, punk." He rubbed mercilessly, squeezing my shaft until I was moaning and arching up toward him. The dildo pressing on my prostate had me leaking like a sieve.

"There's a mighty big load building in here." Sir squeezed my balls hard, tugging them sharply out as they crawled up my shaft. With no warning, my body stiffened. I threw my head back and gasped.

"Sir!"

I yelped as his fingers squeezed a vise around the base of my dick. I gripped the bar stool for all I was worth, shuddering as it felt like Sir squeezed the whole fucking orgasm right back into my nuts. When the urge to come finally passed, I let my head fall forward, panting as I concentrated on the ink snaking up Sir's arms and the thick cushion of fur beneath his shirt. He stepped back and dropped my throbbing dick.

"I'm going out to prune the hedges. Don't move." He gave my ass a nasty slap and stomped out the back door.

Like I was going anywhere, I thought dejectedly. I sat there with my head lowered, watching my dick wave forlornly between my legs, a trail of precum drying on the side of the shaft. I damn well knew better than to move if I ever in this life wanted to come again.

I shot without permission last night. Again. Sir had warned me to control my itchy trigger. He said that if I spurted too soon one more time, I'd rue the day I ever got a hard-on. But I couldn't help it. Just looking at Sir made my dick jump to attention. He was six two, a full five inches taller than my skinny twenty-two-year-old ass. His rock-hard muscular frame was sleeved with biker tattoos and covered with a curly dark pelt that was starting to silver. The pelt matched his short-cropped hair and neatly trimmed beard. The first time I saw his deep-brown eyes glittering at me with fuck lust, I damn near creamed in my jeans.

Sir was meaner than shit when he wanted to fuck. I loved the way he bent me naked over the coffee table and shoved his cock up my ass. The first time he did it, my hole burned open and three strokes later, without me even touching my dick, I was spurting ropy strands onto the polished antique maple. Sir laughed it off, ignoring my now too-tight asshole and jacking off on my face. But after a month of it happening every damn time he fucked me, Sir had run out of patience. Last night had been the last straw.

"Sonofabitch!" he'd roared, when my ass once more clamped down so hard it squeezed him out and wouldn't open up again. Sir threw off the rubber and yanked me down to suck his cock until he spurted all over my still-panting face. He made me sleep on the floor. This morning, as soon as I'd made us breakfast, I'd known my dick and asshole were in for a very rough day. When I'd carried the towels to the laundry room, the lube applicator was sitting on the washing machine, right next to Sir's dildo-decorated training stool.

I could hear him outside in the yard now, watering the hedges and clipping back the new growth. Every once in a while, when he walked by the window, I caught a glimpse of his glistening hair and sweat-soaked T-shirt. My dick twitched again. It was drooping forward, only half-hard, the trail of precum dried into a long, white line. I still felt like I was sitting on a baseball bat. A little bit of friction would sure feel good, just one little up and down to massage my hole's lips. I clenched my sphincter hard around the dildo, craving the sensation, and knowing damn well that even with only a half-hard dick, that one little bit of friction would have me shooting all over the laundry room floor. I kept my feet planted firmly on the bar stool rungs.

The porch door slammed closed and Sir was standing beside me, wiping the sweat off his dripping forehead. My tongue watered, wanting to lick the drop he missed that was running from his wet hairline down into his beard. He grabbed my balls in his dirty hand and squeezed, hard.

"Up and down on the dildo, punk. Fuck your hole good while I play with these pretty little balls." Sir squeezed harder, just the way I loved. Oh fuck, it hurt! With that huge fucking dildo sliding in and out of my hole, the pain in my balls hurt so fucking good! Sir didn't touch my dick, but we both knew he wasn't going to need to. The climax rushed forward so fast I barely had time to choke out "Sir!" I froze in midstroke, gasping as his hand once more clamped ferociously around the base of my dick.

"Good thing I'm fast, punk," he growled, his grip like iron as I panted and shook on my stool. "That jumpy little pecker of yours is going to learn control before it shoots again."

When my breathing finally slowed, he let go and pushed me back down onto the dildo. I held my breath, my eyes closed tight as another urge to come washed through me. Sir leaned forward, his face so close to mine. I felt his breath on my cheek. The stink of his sweat was so overpowering I could almost taste it. I opened my eyes and stared lustfully at him, knowing that if I stuck out my tongue, I could lick the damp trails from his skin. I licked my lips. Sir threw his head back and roared with laughter.

"You got the makings of one fine slutty piece of ass meat," he said, slapping me hard on the thigh. "You just may be worth the time it takes to train you." He walked into the kitchen. I heard the refrigerator door open, then the pop of a beer can as he quenched his thirst. I sat there forlornly on my stool, my cock pointing straight up at my belly, a fresh strand of precum drooling down onto the linoleum.

It was the longest day of my life. Sir went in and out of the house, transforming the yard into the pristine green design he wanted for summer and torturing me until I thought I'd go insane. When he wasn't making me fuck myself over that huge, ass-stretching dildo, he was sucking my tongue and squeezing my balls and stroking my dick with his warm, strong hands. My cock and balls were a deep quivering red, my shaft coated in precum and my balls moving up and down my cock like a pogo stick as he brought me to the brink, over and over again. Sir let me up every hour to stretch and take a piss and drink some water. Then he lubed my hole and I was right back on my fuck stool, with my asshole speared on that fucking dildo and my poor, horny dick teased so hard and so desperate to come I didn't care that I was begging.

"Please, Sir," I pleaded, writhing as he pinched my nipples viciously. "Please, Sir. I need to come so bad." I moaned as he twisted his fingers. He wasn't touching my dick at all this time, just torturing my nipples until they hurt so raw and good tears ran down my cheeks.

"Up," he ordered, his voice low and mean. "Slow and easy,

so you really feel that fake cock sliding through your hole."

I planted my feet and rose, moaning at the delicious feel of the dildo gliding over my asslips. Damn, oh, damn! I loved getting fucked!

"Freeze when you're going to come."

I nodded, unable to speak as the tremors again rippled between my ass and cock and tits. I'd never come just from tit play before. But Sir was really working my nips, twisting and tugging and pinching the tips between his fingernails while I fucked myself up and down on that fucking dildo. I froze in midstroke, my asshole gripping the dildo like a vise as I fought to control the waves suddenly rushing through me.

"Not yet," Sir snarled. I concentrated on his voice, breathing deeply, chanting, *Wait, wait, wait,* over and over in my head as my dick throbbed and I willed myself to do what he wanted. I wanted to come so bad I could hardly stand it. But Sir didn't want me to yet, so I told myself I didn't want to come yet. I didn't, didn't, didn't....

It was a long while before the sensations had passed enough for me to realize I was leaning into Sir's hands. He held me just beneath my pecs, his hands firm and warm and steady, as I rested my head on his salty, wet chest hair. He kept himself perfectly still while I panted and shook in his arms. My dick was waving between my legs, reddish purple and stiff as a steel rod, with precum drooling over the head and down my shaft. But Sir hadn't grabbed my dick, and I still hadn't come! I stared up at him, stunned to realize I'd kept myself from coming all by myself.

"You're learning, punk," he growled. I could see just the edge of a smile touching his lips. "When you're ready, slide back down on your dildo and think about how you did that."

I thought, while he mowed the lawn and transplanted the

new bougainvillea and replaced the rocks around the koi pond. I thought even harder as he stroked my dick and I licked the sweat from his pits, concentrating on the sound of his voice, just his voice, as he ordered me up and down on my dildo. When he was gone again, I tipped my head back, breathing slowly and deeply, listening to him put the mower and yard tools away and close up the garage. I'd never been that horny in my life. I'd do anything, anything to please him!

Sir walked back in the room and shut the door in behind him. Even from my perch on my stool, I could smell his sweat. My swollen cock jutted up hard between my legs, desperate for relief. Sir leaned against the dryer and stripped off his shirt, shorts, and salt-stained, dirty jock. He reached in his pocket and took out a rubber. My mouth watered as he unrolled the thin sheath over his huge, swollen cock. My asshole twitched as he squeezed lube on his palm and slathered it on until the rubber glistened like it was covered with sweat, too. Then Sir slapped his hand on the dryer.

"Hands here. Bend over with your legs spread and your hole open. And don't you even dream of coming until I say so!"

My dick gave one quick, ferocious twitch as I rose up off my stool. Then I was bent over with my ass waving in the air, begging for Sir's cock. He thrust into me fast and deep. I moaned so hard my throat hurt. His dick felt so good, so fucking, fucking good inside me. I tried to concentrate. I gasped as the climax surged forward, choking on my startled "Sir!" as his hand clamped around me.

"S-sorry, Sir!" I gasped. "I almost h-had it!"

"Try again," he growled, squeezing until I moaned at the pain. "I'm going to come up your ass, punk." I groaned as he thrust forward again. "I...am...going...to...fuck...fuck... FUCK...your...fucking...punk...ass!"

With each thrust, my balls wanted to crawl up my dick. But after a whole day sitting on that huge, fucking dildo, my hole was stretched so wide I wasn't squeezing Sir out. He fucked me until I was so raw and so desperate my whole body felt like it was on fire. Then suddenly, he laughed low in his throat.

"Oh, yeah, punk. I'm gonna shoot up your loose punk hole. Your ass is sucking me off good. Those nice loose lips are pulling a real good come from my balls." He thrust hard into my joy spot. As I yelled out, "SIR!" he grabbed my hips and yanked me up onto my toes, pulling my ass so wide and deep onto his cock I almost felt his dick on my tonsils. He ground into my joy spot, his dick surging as he roared out, "Now, punk!"

I yelled as oceans of cum erupted through my dick. My asshole clamped down as hard as it could around the huge cock buried deep in my ass, trying to squeeze and clench over his thick, stiff meat while my dick spurted like a fire hose. Finally, it couldn't keep him out! The come seemed to last forever as my ass worked itself over Sir's dick, milking the most incredible orgasm of my life from the root of Sir's balls.

I could barely stand when he let me down. My legs shook as he held me to him. The low rumble of his laugh vibrated through me.

"You've got the beginnings of a fine, trained asshole punk." He kissed me roughly on the back of my neck, then reached around and took my sticky, softening dick in his calloused hand. "Your hole felt real good on my dick. With some serious training, you'll be able to scratch my dick just fine."

I shook as Sir squeezed the last drop of cum up through my cock tube. I looked over at the dildo waving on the bar stool, moaning as Sir's dick slid free. Yes, sir, I was going to love training my itchy trigger!

# DOCTOR'S ORDERS

## K. Lynn

The small emergency room was quiet for a Wednesday night. No new patients had wandered in for over two hours and David was wondering if he was going to make it through the rest of his shift without a case. He figured that was why his attending was currently missing in action. Dr. Stewart had said something about paging him if there was an emergency, and then he left in the elevator. If David had to guess, he would bet the older man was wasting time down in the cafeteria. It seemed to be his go-to place when he got bored.

David didn't have that option. Instead, he had to rely on whatever the vending machine in the lounge was stocked with. Most people thought doctors had the healthiest diets imaginable, but they were wrong. Cookies, soda, and the occasional pack of crackers were often his meal for the night shift. Tonight's choice was chips, likely stale, but at least it would cure his hunger. That was, if the cursed machine would let go of the bag. He banged his hand against the metal side and finally the chips dropped. He was just reaching inside to retrieve his food when his pager went off. Looked like the ER had a case for him after all.

Shelly was at the desk when he returned, raising an eyebrow at him as he crunched his way through the remaining chips in his bag. David tried to swallow his last bite quick.

"What?" he asked, wadding up his trash and throwing it into the can sitting beside the sink. "I was hungry."

"Uh-huh." She watched him as he went through the motions of washing his hands. "And running down to the cafeteria for an apple would kill you?"

David decided to ignore her. She was always after him to eat healthy, chiding him like she was his mother. Well, she was old enough, but he dare not mention that.

"Did you call me down here to complain about my eating habits, or do we have a case?" He dried his hands on a paper towel and discarded it.

"Got a stitch job in Room Four," she said, handing over a patient folder. "Guy got into a bar fight and busted his forehead open."

David grimaced. Head wounds always bled like a bitch. "I said I wanted some excitement tonight. Guess I shouldn't have pressed my luck, huh?"

Shelly winked at him as he passed by her, heading to the specified area. David gave a quick knock on the door to let his patient know he was there, then walked inside. The man sitting on the gurney looked rough. There was no other way to describe it. Rivets of dried blood marked his left cheek and the wound on his forehead hadn't stopped bleeding all the way. He still wore his leather jacket, as if he was just stopping by for a visit and would be on his way soon. It certainly added to his tough-guy image, if nothing else.

"Mr. Barton?" David asked, double-checking the folder and looking back up.

The man gave a nod. "It's Steve."

"All right, Steve. I'm Dr. Woods, nice to meet you." David set the folder aside on the room's only table. He gave Steve a smile as he went over to the cabinet and pulled out a pair of gloves. "Looks like you got yourself into some trouble there."

Steve gave a grunt. "Bar fight. Took a hit when I shouldn't have."

David nodded, grabbing a handful of alcohol wipes and dumping them on the bed beside his patient. "You might want to take off your jacket. Make yourself more comfortable."

Steve narrowed his eyes at David, but finally seemed to agree. He pulled first one arm, then the other out of his jacket sleeves. David could see the man's bulging muscles straining against the short sleeves of his white T-shirt, a light line of a scar peeking out underneath his right one. If they were somewhere else, in a club or a bar, David would have been on him fast. The slight hint of danger did something to him. He could feel a flare of arousal run through his body, but he tried to keep his mind on more professional matters.

Steve didn't seem to notice the close examination, just set his jacket on the pillow beside him and let his hands rest on the mattress. David cleared his throat, telling himself that he had a job to do. He tore open one of the alcohol packets and stepped nearer to Steve. "I need to clean up the blood so I can take a look at your wound. You'll likely need stitches."

"Wouldn't be the first time," Steve said, tightening his grip on the mattress edge when David gave his cheek a swipe with the cold alcohol pad.

"So, what was the damage on the other guy, if he got you this bad?" he asked, cleaning up the dried blood.

Steve closed his eyes, tilting his head to the side so that David had better access. "He's probably passed out at home by now. I laid him out with a punch and his buddies had to drag him outside and put him in the backseat of their car."

"Well, I guess he got lucky then," David said, giving a short laugh as he finished cleaning up around the wound. It still wasn't sealing up, so he knew he'd have to stitch it closed so it could heal properly.

David dumped the bloody pads into the trashcan on the other side of the room and stripped off his dirty gloves. He picked up the room phone and called to the front desk.

"Yeah?" Shelly answered, sounding tired.

"Is that how you're supposed to answer the phone?"

"It is when I know it's you calling," she said, not the least bit apologetic. "What do you need?"

"Suture kit and a dose of Lidocaine, if you wouldn't mind." He looked over at Steve, who was hunched over and looking at the floor. David saw that his wound was starting to bleed again. "Uh, better put a hurry on that. Doesn't look like it's going to clot on its own." He didn't give Shelly a chance to answer, just hung up the phone and grabbed a gauze pad before he headed back to the bed.

"Look up," he said, causing Steve to raise his head. He pressed the gauze against the wound. "Hold this against your head until I can get a suture kit. Don't want you to bleed out on me." David flashed a smirk to let Steve know he was joking.

He grabbed the rolling stool that was sitting beside the table and sat down. "The nurse shouldn't be long."

Steve gave a short nod then grimaced in pain. David couldn't help but be intrigued by this guy. Steve didn't seem very comfortable in a medical setting and it made David wonder why. Had he had a bad experience before? Judging by the thin white lines he saw along Steve's underarm and the prior scar he had seen, it wasn't the first time the man had gotten injured.

"So, what brought this all on, if you don't mind me asking?"

Steve didn't immediately answer, just ducked his head down a bit like he was embarrassed. It wasn't going to help the bleeding any if he kept doing that.

"Come on, it can't be that bad." Steve looked up at him, a faint blush coloring his cheeks. "Okay, maybe it can."

Steve remained silent, but David was willing to wait him out. He grabbed Steve's file and started filling out the information he'd need for processing. Might as well use the time for something productive. Finally, David's patience was rewarded and Steve started talking.

"It was stupid." David looked over at him, waiting for him to continue. "The guy started playing this song on the jukebox, and I told him to shut it off. We got into it, and then this happened," he said, waving his right hand at his forehead.

David nodded, continuing his paperwork. "I've had a few of those nights."

"And I can just imagine what the guys I ride with are going to say when they find out." Steve pulled the dressing off his forehead and gave it a look. He grimaced at the blood then pressed it back against his wound. "I've got scars from knife fights, broke three bones falling out a window and even took a bullet to the leg once. Now every time somebody looks at me they'll be reminded that I'm some kind of pussy who can't stand hearing George Michael."

David's pen pulled hard across the page at the revelation. Fuck, he'd have to write the whole damn thing over again. But he couldn't worry about that now because his mind was too busy processing what he'd just heard. There were very few bars left in the immediate area. Most closed down when the recession hit and the crowds either gathered at one of the local restaurants instead or they headed thirty miles out of town to find a place that still served good liquor. Of the remaining bars, David knew of only one that kept George Michael in constant rotation.

He looked over to Steve. "Did you happen to get into this fight over at Randy's Place?" he asked, trying to keep his voice steady.

Steve stilled at the question, his expression going from open to guarded in a flash. "How'd you know that?"

David let out a laugh, feeling a rush of happiness and desire run through him all at once. Of course the gay resident on duty would get the only hot, gay biker in a fifty-mile radius. It was just that kind of night. David could feel his cock growing heavy with arousal and he knew his scrubs would not keep it secret for long.

"Because I head out there every Saturday night when I'm not working." David could see a change in Steve's demeanor as soon as the realization hit him. Steve went relaxed again, a tentative smile playing on his lips.

"Yeah?"

"But I haven't seen you around there before." David's tongue darted out and he licked his lower lip. "I'd remember if I had."

"I don't get away from the guys that much," Steve said, widening his legs where he sat on the table. It seemed he was taking notice of David as much as the young resident was taking notice of Steve. "They're cool with it, you know, but they wouldn't be comfortable in a place like that."

David was about to respond, but he was interrupted by a knock at the door. He grabbed the folder and set it on his lap to cover his growing erection as Shelly came inside with the tray of requested medical supplies.

"Sorry it took so long," she said, setting everything down. "The suture kits weren't where they were supposed to be."

"That's okay," David said, clearing his throat. "Mr. Barton is still doing fine, aren't you Mr. Barton?"

"Doing fine," Steve said, removing the gauze and looking at it. "Might've even stopped bleeding."

"Do you need me to help or...?" Shelly began, but David cut her off.

"No, no, I've got it." He still didn't rise from his seat, which caused a look of confusion to cross her face. "Seriously, we've got this covered."

Shelly narrowed her eyes at him then glanced over at Steve. When she looked back at David she still didn't seem to understand what was going on, but she let it drop. "Okay, I'll be at the desk if you need me. Mr. Barton can check out when you're done."

Steve gave her a nod. "Appreciate it."

Shelly turned to go and David didn't let out a breath until she closed the door behind her. He turned quick to look over at Steve when the other man gave a quick laugh.

"She's got your number."

"I'm sure she does," David sighed, putting the folder back on the table before he stood. "But I've got more important issues at the moment. Let's get you sewn up."

He put himself into professional mode again. As much as this guy got him worked up, he was still a doctor and he had a job to do. David was methodical, going through the motions of washing his hands, putting on his gloves, and filling the syringe with local anesthetic before he approached the bed. Looking at the wound, he could tell that it was beginning to clot up, but it wouldn't close all the way without help.

"This is going to numb the area so I can get the stitches in," he said, holding up the needle. Steve tilted his head up so that David could have free access to work. He pressed the needle in, noticing the slight flinch from Steve as he did, and applied the local.

He pulled the needle out and walked over to dispose of it. "We'll have to wait a minute for that to take full effect and then I can start putting in the stitches."

David busied himself with getting the suture kit ready. Once he had everything put together, he carried it over to Steve. David prodded the skin around the wound with his free hand. "Do you feel anything?"

"Just a little bit of pressure. Feels weird," Steve said, trying to bunch up his forehead.

"Good, means it's working. Try to relax and it'll be over in a minute." David steadied himself as the needle pierced Steve's skin.

He worked methodically, losing himself in the action as he closed the wound. Steve's breath remained steady as David worked, but the same could not be said of the young resident. Pressed this close to Steve, he could smell the faint aroma of sweat, cologne, and leather from his nearby jacket. He hadn't noticed it before, probably because he wouldn't allow himself to, but now that he knew Steve was open to the possibility it was like David's senses were on overload. And he almost missed a stitch when his half-hard cock brushed against the rough denim of Steve's jeans. He tried to cover his reaction, but by the look Steve gave him he knew he was busted. However, neither man mentioned it as the treatment continued and soon the young resident was finished, tying off the stitch where he'd cut it.

"Almost finished," he said, dumping his kit onto the medical tray and opening the cabinet to look for a dressing. David tried to clear his mind and regain control over his body. He was a doctor, this was his patient, and whatever he was thinking was not going to happen.

With shaky hands, he ripped open the dressing packet and discarded the trash on his way back to the bed. "I'll write you a prescription for some pain relievers and a supply of these," he said, pressing the adhesive bandage onto Steve's forehead. "Keep it dry and covered for a few days. And take the pain medication as needed. It's going to bruise tomorrow, but that's normal."

He turned away before he could embarrass himself any further. "I'll write you a prescription and you can pick it up in the pharmacy." He jotted some discharge notes in Steve's folder. "And you're all taken care of," he said, turning back to his patient, but Steve was not where he had left him. He was, instead, mere inches away from Steve and coming closer.

"Now it's my turn to take care of you," Steve said, grabbing David by the waist and spinning him around so that his back was pressed against the exam table and Steve was pressed against his front.

David could feel the rough texture of Steve's growing erection against his own and his breath hitched at the contact. Steve seemed to take this as permission to continue. The biker ground himself against David, forcing both pain and pleasure to rush up from his groin.

"This isn't appropriate," David said, his breath coming in gasps each time Steve pressed against him.

"You trying to say you're not interested?" Steve asked, tightening his grip on David's sides. David wondered if he'd have finger bruises tomorrow, considering how firm the hold was.

And he couldn't deny that he was interested, couldn't think clearly enough to form the lie. "We could get caught."

"Might, but we won't," Steve said, pulling back a little. "Not if I'm quick."

His hands fell from David's sides and instead concentrated on the knot in the front of the young resident's scrub pants. It took him no time to get them loose and David only had a second to think about what was happening before Steve's right hand was inside the scrubs, under the elastic of his underwear, and had a firm hold on David's cock.

David arched up into the touch. "Holy fuck!" He grabbed for something to brace himself against and that happened to be Steve's muscular shoulders. His fingers tightened against the material of Steve's shirt, digging in.

"Already on the edge," Steve said, giving David's cock a squeeze. He put his left hand against David's back and pulled him in, their bodies a bit off-center so that Steve's denim-covered bulge was rubbing against David's thigh.

"How fast do you think I can get you off?" Steve asked, rutting against David and tightening his grip at the same time.

David buried his face into Steve's shoulder, breathing in the smell of sweat and cologne as he felt the man's muscles bunch under his touch. He was lost to the feeling, not able to think or protest, but merely along for the ride.

Steve didn't keep up his conversation, instead focused on his task. Up and down David's cock, his firm grip making David grow harder and closer to release. Steve's breath was starting to quicken as well, working himself against David's leg. He wondered if Steve was going to come along with him.

David's body rocked into the touch; each cycle up his length and back got the blood pumping faster and David could tell he was close, almost there. He tried to warn Steve, but all he managed was a muttered, "Damn, oh damn," before he was coming wet and warm in his underwear, spilling over Steve's hand. And Steve rode the orgasm with him, rutting and pushing until he gave a shutter and a grunt. It seemed David wasn't the only one getting off.

His cock started softening in Steve's grasp, but the movements up and down the shaft remained steady until it was clear David was done. Steve gave him one last squeeze, almost too tight as a flash of pain ran up David's body, and then the biker pulled his hand free.

David remained pressed against the bed, breath heavy and his scrub pants sticky against the wet material of his underwear. He watched, silent, as Steve went over to the sink and ran his hands under the faucet to clean himself up a bit.

Then Steve was nearing him again, leaning close as his breath tickled David's ear. "See you around, Doc." His arm reached around David to grab his leather jacket and then he was moving away, grabbing his folder and heading to the door.

Then he was gone, closing the door behind him and leaving David alone, breath still hitching and pants sticky and ruined. He didn't know how he was going to get out without being noticed, having to explain why he was in such a state, but he wasn't thinking of that. The only thing running through his mind was Steve. Against everything he was taught, he hoped the biker might get into another fight just so David could guarantee that he'd see him again. After all, he was pretty good at patching him up.

# I DIDN'T WANT DANGER

## Charlie Purcell

I watched the milky white clouds in my coffee disappear and reappear in a slow circle. The coffee was already cold, and more creamer would only make it colder.

The waitress glared at me. She knew I needed a refill, but she kept serving all the other customers first. I guess she knew that I didn't belong here. The poor side of town. I wasn't really a part of this world.

Finally, she walked over and poured a little more coffee into my cup.

"Thanks," I said.

She nodded. She had bright-red lips that distracted from the rest of her sour face. She probably would've looked prettier if she smiled.

I'd been waiting at this diner for the last twenty minutes. My leg was shaking like crazy. It got like that whenever I was nervous. I just sat there, trying to keep my brain completely empty. I didn't want any trouble. I just wanted to get in, get out, get it over with.

"Are you Reggie?" a voice asked behind me. He sounded like his vocal chords had suffered from a few too many drags on a cigarette: gruff and just a little bit jaded. It didn't take me long to realize that this guy was the one I'd been waiting for.

I spun around on the stool. The stool made a long, labored grinding noise, rusted metal twisting around rusted metal. It was the kind of sound that almost made your ears get tetanus.

This diner was ancient. It had been a fixture of downtown Kingman at least since the early fifties. I expected a little wear and tear. Heck, I chose this place because it wasn't on the upscale side of things. But I didn't expect their furniture to look and sound like torture devices.

I also didn't expect the guy who was standing right in front of me. Loan sharks are supposed to be big fat guys with jowls and ill-fitting tracksuits. They were extras on "The Sopranos." They weren't, well, gorgeous.

"You're Reggie, right?" he asked me again.

"Sure," I said. Technically, my name was Tom, but I wasn't going to give this guy any information about me. This was supposed to be quick and painless. Meet and greet, money exchanged, and then BAM, I'd never see his face again. But my sore tailbone and ice-cold coffee told me that we were already running nearly a half hour late.

"Thought it was you," he said. "You mind if we move some-where more private?"

I didn't know what he was getting at, until he tilted his head toward the booth in the far corner of the diner. It was just as dirty and run-down as the rest of the diner, but it was far away from any eavesdroppers.

"I can ask," I said, and turned toward the waitress.

She glared at us—well, mostly me—and nodded her head over toward the corner of the diner. She smirked a little, too, as if to say, *No funny business, guys.*

I brought along my unfinished cup of coffee. It was likely to remain unfinished, but I didn't want to be rude.

As we headed over to our private corner, I got a good look of this loan shark. Brad, by the way. Brad was his name. But it was probably just as made-up as Reggie.

He lumbered to the table, swinging his huge, tattooed arms like an animal. He rippled with muscles. I could see each one flex under his tight black shirt. He was a good three inches taller than me, with long, thick legs packed inside a pair of old, gray jeans.

I tried my hardest not to look at his backside, which swayed while he walked. He had the body of a boxer, or an MMA fighter, or some Greek statue that I had to study in college. Underneath his grubby outfit and dark, angry tattoos, his body was basically perfect.

"You gonna keep checking me out, or you gonna have a seat?" he asked.

Damn. This was exactly what I didn't want to happen. I didn't want to show weakness. Why couldn't he have looked like some gone-to-seed construction worker or fat mob stereotype? Why'd he have to be so hot?

I sat across from him.

Should I fold my hands? Should I leave them at my sides? I fidgeted a little, until I could tell that he was getting impatient.

I waited for the loan shark to say something. Brad, I kept telling myself. I waited for Brad to say something. He wasn't just a loan shark. He was a human being. A large, rippling human being with thick veins that roped around his forearms.

Damn. I was doing it again.

He didn't say anything. Was he waiting for me to initiate the conversation? Instead, he pushed his fingers through the tattered horizontal blinds and let some light stream into the diner. I could see a small square of the surrounding neighborhood through the hole. This used to be the nice part of town, until the train got rerouted and the old townhouses started to crumble into slums.

Swirls of dust danced through the stream of light. I drank one more sip of my coffee, even though it was cold and bitter. It was quickly becoming clear that Brad wasn't going to officially introduce himself, or say anything at all really. It was a power play, I guess.

"So you live around here?" I asked. He looked at me with his gray eyes. I was scared, but only a little. He seemed like the kind of guy who didn't answer questions. "I've only been on this side of town a couple times," I added. "There's a lot of history here. I think..."

He snapped his knuckles once, just once, but it was loud and violent. His fingers were thick and rough. For a second, I imagined all the things he could do with those hands. I imagined them grabbing my shoulders and pulling me close to his thick, muscled chest. God, he was so warm. He held me like no other man could hold me. His raw power throbbed out of him, radiating warmth and electricity wherever he touched me. God, he was so...

Christ, I was doing it again. I quickly shook the thoughts out of my head and turned to look back at the window. Why did this stranger have so much power over me? I'd never seen him before. I'd never dated anyone who even remotely looked like him. The goatee, the tattoos, the wild, unwashed hair. He was the exact opposite of the kind of guy I usually dated.

Maybe it was the danger of this whole situation. Maybe I was just flustered because I was meeting with an actual criminal.

"Let's talk money," he finally said. I guess he got tired of the awkward glances and silence. A fly buzzed around his side of the table, and he pounded his fist right where it landed. No more buzzing.

"Yes," I said. "I have everything right here. I..."

I quickly pulled the envelope of cash out of my front pocket and slid it on the table.

He glared at me like I was the biggest idiot of the century. "Put that away," he growled.

I slid my arm over the envelope and pulled it back toward my edge of the table.

"Look, buddy," he said, "I'm cutting you some slack because this isn't even your debt. It's your uncle's. And I know your uncle. He's a real prick. So I respect that you're helping out your family like this, but if you draw any more unnecessary attention to us, I will walk right out of here and reclaim my debt another way."

I'd seen enough gangster movies. That meant kneecaps.

"I understand," I mumbled.

"Great," he said. "Now tell me some cutesy story about your life and slowly slide the cash over to me."

Yet again, I was speechless. I just had to say something. It didn't even need to be real, just some verbal garbage to distract the other diners from the cash exchange. But my brain was completely blank and I could not think of a single thing to say.

"I, um, I drove here about forty minutes ago and ordered some coffee," I said. "I waited for you for a little bit and then..."

"You're really bad at this. I hope you know that," he said. And he laughed. The buff, grungy loan shark allowed his gray eyes to lighten up to a watery blue, his mouth to crinkle upward, and his throat to let out a loud, hearty laugh.

It terrified me, just like everything else about him.

The money envelope was now halfway across the table, and

my hand was still on it. I was waiting for him to take it from me, but he wouldn't. He kept laughing and gazing through the blinds into the sunlight outside.

"You know," he finally said, "I wasn't expecting someone who looks like you. You really don't look like a schoolteacher. You seem much too athletic and fit."

My veins froze into jets of ice. I couldn't breathe. How could this guy know that I was a schoolteacher? I didn't even give him my real name.

"You look surprised," he said. "Don't worry. It's all part of my job. You don't think I'd do business with a complete stranger, do you? I always check up on my...partners. Your real name's Tom, right? Tom Brantley. Not Reggie, like your uncle told me over the phone. You teach history at the private school uptown. You enjoy going to the movie theater by yourself, presumably so you don't have to make small talk with anybody while the film is rolling. I appreciate that. And of course, you have never, never exchanged money with a businessman like myself."

The entire time he talked to me, he never gave me eye contact. Instead, he looked out the window, letting the sun catch his eyes at just the right angle. They looked cold, his eyes. Cold chunks of blue in the bright sunlight. I was drawn to them. I was drawn to HIM, but the voice in my head told me to run as far away as possible.

Suddenly, he turned his gaze to look directly at me. The blinds snapped shut and the light disappeared. "You're single, too," he added. "You live alone. Which surprises me, I guess. A handsome guy like you. I guess you haven't found the right girl yet."

His last comment surprised me. Actually, it did more than that. It almost punched me in the face. This guy knew everything about me. He knew my movie-watching habits! But he didn't know that I was gay? That was a major part of my life, and a well-documented one, too. There was no way that he would let that piece of information slip past him.

"Or guy," he added.

And there it was. If I didn't know better, I would have thought that he was flirting with me. But no. That couldn't be happening. He was a tough guy. A criminal.

"Excuse me, you two. Thought about ordering anything?" That was the waitress, as pleasant as always. Somehow, it looked like her lipstick was even redder than before. Pretty soon, she'd be glowing in the dark.

I was about to ask for a bit more coffee to warm my cup, when Brad's hand quickly dropped on top of mine. I had forgotten about the envelope of cash peeking out from under my grip. His hand rested on mine, and because his palm was so wide, it completely obscured the envelope.

"We'll need a few more minutes," Brad said. He smiled at her with a two-second "go away" smile.

The waitress looked down at us strangely. She had the decency not to glance down at our hands. And she walked away.

"Sorry about that, Tom," he said. "Don't want to rile up any more suspicion."

"I understand," I said. But what I didn't understand was why he wasn't pulling his hand away. Instead, he left it cradling mine. His fingers weren't as rough as they looked. In fact, they were almost tender. Before I realized what was happening, he started moving his thumb in widening circles, feeling the back of my hand. Feeling my scars and veins. After almost a minute, it became obvious that he wasn't letting go.

"You're still touching me," I muttered.

"You're still letting me," he said, his voice firm and assured.

I pulled my hand away.

He grabbed the envelope of cash and stashed it in his pocket.

For just a second, Brad's jaw line quivered, as if he were clenching and unclenching his teeth. It was an emotional reveal, a moment of weakness, and I could tell that he instantly regretted showing that to me. He looked away again.

I took a closer look at the dark tattoo winding its way along the side of his neck. I couldn't tell if it was barbed wire or some sort of thorny vine.

He wasn't going to say anything else, so I started, "So you don't want to count th—"

"You're single, right?" he asked.

"Yes," I said. "You know that. You told me you knew that."

"Yeah," he said. "Just checking. Me too"

I wasn't sure if I believed him.

I looked at him for a long time. I forgot about the tattoos, and the thin scar along his right cheekbone, and the way he let his hair just hang around his face. He still scared me. He was still dangerous, but there was something more to him, too. He almost seemed…incomplete.

"Let me tell you what you want to do to me right now," he said.

And just like that, the vulnerability was gone. The gentleness. He was like an animal again. And he wanted to lash out.

"Sure," I said. "What do I want to do to you?" I feared what he was about to say, but I hungered for it, too. What did I want to do to him? God, I couldn't even describe it.

"You want to fix me," he said. "You want to, like, take me back to your place, clean me up, get me a damn haircut and take me to the mall."

I didn't know what to say.

"I don't like when people look at me like that," he said. "I'm happy the way I am. I'm fucking ecstatic."

"How was I looking at you?" I asked.

"Like a leper. I'm not, you know. I'm good."

I reached out to grab his hand again, but this time he pulled away. "I'm sorry. I..."

Brad let out another big, hearty laugh, like what he just said was the funniest thing in the world. He clutched his stomach. It was loud enough for the waitress to poke her head out of the kitchen and check us out again.

I wasn't sure what to do, so I started laughing too.

"Naw, man," Brad said. "We're good. We're good."

By this point in our meeting, I had no idea how to read him. One minute he would lash out at me; the next minute he would pull everything back and make a big joke out of it. This was like a big game to him. Did he like me? Was he even gay? My body was on edge and I could feel my nerves dance right below my skin.

"Brad," I said.

"I should probably tell you that that's not my real name, either," he said. I waited for him to tell me what his real name was, but he didn't add anything. Instead, he pulled the money back out of his pocket and handed it back to me. He wasn't sly about it either. Anyone in the diner could tell that we were exchanging money.

"Here," he said. "You're a teacher. You probably need this more than I do."

"But what about my uncle's debt?"

At that, he glanced at me sideways and curled his mouth into a sinister smile. "You know there are other ways to pay off his debt."

I was offended. I was pissed off. What a jackass! I tossed the envelope back to him, dropped a couple loose bucks on the table for our waitress, and walked right out the door.

When I got out into the parking lot, I realized that there were only two cars in the lot: mine and Brad's. No one else was here. All the other customers had already left. The waitress probably parked out back.

I fumbled with my keys. I couldn't get out of there fast enough. How could he even suggest that? I was a nice guy. A smart guy. I would never sleep with a jackass like that, no matter how he made me feel.

He was probably looking at me right now, through those vertical blinds, chuckling to himself that he scared off another one. Whatever. The debt was paid. I never had to see him again.

"Hey, Reggie! I mean Tom! Hey, Tom!" The voice was coming from right behind me.

I was wrong. He wasn't watching me from the diner. He had followed me outside.

"Go away," I said.

Damn! Why did I keep dropping my keys?

He grabbed me and spun me around. God, he was strong. He held me by my shoulders and forced me to look at him.

"I shouldn't have said that," he said. "I realize how it came across. I'm sorry. I... This has nothing to do with money. I just..."

It was a strange combination. His body was so strong and forceful, but he couldn't even finish his sentences. He was struggling to find the words to tell me.

"Yeah," I said. "I figured you probably didn't mean anything by it. It's just that, well, you're dangerous. I don't want to get mixed up in your world."

He smiled again. It was that lopsided smile. It lit up his face. "I think you do," he said.

The decision was up to me now. I knew he was bad news. Every fiber in my body told me he was trouble. But maybe a little trouble was what I wanted.

I poked my keys into the hole and unlocked my car door.

Brad stood there, looking at me.

"Well?" I asked. "Wanna come back to my place?"

He shook his head no. "Too far."

Without saying anything else, he grabbed my wrist and started pulling me back toward the restaurant. Instead of going in the main doors, he led me around the back, where its bathrooms hid amongst the mesquite trees. It was dark back there, and secluded too. No one could hear us.

As soon as the bathroom door clicked shut behind us, Brad placed his left hand on my neck and pulled me close. He kissed me before I could fight it, his sharp stubble colliding with my flesh and adding just a little bit of pain to the pleasure of his warm, parted lips.

After a few seconds, I heard Brad's zipper slide open. He was a businessman, after all. He cut to the chase. I kissed him once more, and then dropped to my knees to check out the goods.

The scent of his groin was strong and musky. I opened my mouth wide and swallowed, taking his thick member down my throat. His dick throbbed, and my tongue could trace the outlines of the pulsing veins that roped across it. I hooked my finger into the belt loop of his jeans, pulling them down even farther. I wanted to see skin. My left hand held tightly to his muscular asscheek as my tongue explored his shaft. His knees buckled for an instant, but just for an instant, as I began to suck a little harder. I feasted on him. I delighted in the natural, earthy tastes that danced throughout my mouth.

Brad grabbed a handful of my hair and pulled me off his

cock. Like everything else he did, his movement was forceful and direct. His hard dick popped out of my mouth, leaving a trail of saliva and precum on the edge of my lips. I licked the head just one more time before he could stop me.

"Over the sink," he said. It wasn't a question. It wasn't even a full sentence.

I did as I was told. I spun around and put both hands on the countertop. It was caked in dust, but otherwise clean. His hands went around my waist, and unhooked my belt. For a second, I reveled in the feel of his muscular arms surrounding me. My pants instantly slid below my ass; I could tell that he'd unbuckled a few belts before.

"Not bad," he said, pinching my asscheek.

I grunted.

His rough fingers grabbed each cheek and pulled them apart. He slid one finger up and down my crack, slowly running circles around my ring. Brad paused a second, and then lowered himself to face my hole, shoving his nose where I could feel it. He sniffed. His stubble again scraped against my skin. I fell forward, propping up most of my weight by my elbows. His tongue poked into my hole, gliding in circles, sliding its rough surface over everything I had to offer. His tongue entered me and I could feel its thrusts until, all too quickly, he pulled away.

I heard the rustle of fabric, and then the click of an opened container of lube. It felt like hours before he shoved his slick fingers into my ass. First one finger, and then three, deeper and deeper. My balls throbbed. And before I knew it, it wasn't his finger inside me, but his cock. One hand guided it right to the danger zone, his cockhead warm as it pressed into my ring.

I arched my back and readied myself. *Here it comes.* He entered with a groan.

He was overpowering me. There was too much of him, but

he kept sliding inside, more and more of him, until I felt filled to capacity. His free hand was pinching my nipple, a painful surprise that sent a single shiver throughout my body. He began to thrust. The counters shook and the sinks almost dislodged from the wall.

*Oh god! Oh Brad!*

I almost shouted out his name, but I knew it was fake, and in this intense moment of pleasure, I didn't want a single thing to seem like a lie. "Oh god!" I shouted.

He hammered me, again and again, each time feeling deeper and more powerful. A breath caught in my throat. He was rough, rougher than I expected. He dove into me, so hard and deep. He almost cracked me open. I almost gave up. I almost couldn't handle it, but he continued, and I discovered new thresholds of experience. The rougher it got, the more I wanted it. He tightened his grip on my nipple and I knew to prepare myself. He shot a powerful, steady stream straight into me, and I was filled even more. I felt his load shoot through my insides, uniting us, tying us together for just an instant. When he pulled out, I was exhausted and fulfilled. The last bits of him trickled down my thigh.

All my strength left me and I collapsed onto the bathroom counter. It gave a little under my weight—we had certainly knocked a few bolts loose—but it held firm. "Oh god," I said once more.

He wrapped his arm around me and pulled me completely to my feet. While I stood there, moist and exhausted, he ran his fingers up and down my torso. His fingertips left thin trails of electricity in their wake.

Brad laughed.

"What's so funny?" I asked. My voice sounded rougher, raspier than usual.

"Nothing," he said. "I guess this is what you get for coming to this side of town."

"I guess it is," I said, laughing a little, too.

He kissed me once more, his tongue lingering on mine.

After a quick good-bye, Brad cleaned himself up and left. I knew I wouldn't see him again. I wasn't part of his world. He wasn't part of mine. For this one brief encounter, we were connected, but that was never going to last.

I watched him leave, his ass once again packed tightly in those dirty jeans. He didn't just walk away, he lumbered. He had power in every movement. Before I knew it, he was gone, and the last traces of his musky scent disappeared. He probably wouldn't even remember this in a month, in a week, in a day. He wouldn't remember, but I certainly would. For this one afternoon, I asked for trouble. And when trouble came, I liked it.

# TAKING AUSTIN

## Martha Davis

I looked back over my shoulder then plopped down in the first available bar stool and ordered a beer. The bar was dim, smoky, the heat turned up a tad too high. Three older people navigated a pool table in one corner; a straight couple felt each other up under the table in another. Two waitresses wiped down glasses and gossiped at the other end of the bar. You'd think a place called Brimstone would be way more badass.

The bartender pulled my drink from the tap but when I reached for it, he pressed his knuckles against the glass and slid it out of reach.

"Nuh-uh. ID first."

I reached in the back pocket of my jeans and pulled out my wallet, yanked my driver's license out and chucked it in his direction.

He took it to a computer monitor behind the cash register, pressed a few buttons, smiled slowly. "Austin Gregory?"

"I'm legal."

"Barely."

He tossed the ID back with a fancy wrist flick while simultaneously sliding my beer back in reach.

I gulped half of it down at once and refused to cough when the burn hit the back of my throat. Where did he make this shit, his backyard?

The bartender checked me out without caring if I saw, assessed me up and down, judging me like he knew me. I snorted and returned the favor, scanning him just as hard. He was blond with curly hair, tall and muscular, overdressed for a minimum wage bartender, wearing a starched white shirt and gray pants. The only deviances from hardcore lame-ass office drone were a name tag on his right breast pocket reading SNAKE and a black tie printed with little skulls and crossbones.

Our eyes met. His were as gold as the locks of his hair, glistening like molten metal in the dim light. They almost didn't look human.

His smile broadened. "You have permission to suck my cock."

What the fuck? "Sorry, dude, you ain't my type."

"Oh, I am most definitely your type."

The bartender turned to his right and smiled fondly at the approaching redheaded waitress.

"P.D. is coming, Boss."

"I know Satrinah." He stroked the line of her jaw and winked. "I can smell them."

Snake looked in my direction. "Ready to tell me what you did?"

"I didn't do shit!"

His eyes roved over me again, taking in the tight jeans torn at the knee, the black leather jacket and old Poison concert T-shirt I'd found in a thrift store.

"Got any tattoos?"

"A couple. Why?"

"Any on your hairy ass?"

"Fuck you!"

"I said you could suck my cock. You haven't earned a fuck yet."

"What is wrong with you? Have you lost your fucking mind?"

I got up to leave about the same time two police officers walked through the front door. Snake reached over the bar and took me by the elbow. "Sit down and keep making small talk. Try not to look so damned scared."

He poured me another beer. "Here. Drink. This one is a little more refined. Better for your young, untried palate."

The officers had a short talk with the bouncer who pointed in our direction.

"An owl."

"An owl?"

"Yes, I have an owl tattooed on my butt so I can be a wiseass forever. Why are you so curious? Do ass tattoos get you off?"

"Just interested."

"What are you? Some kind of wannabe badass?"

He snorted.

"Are you the owner?" The taller of the two officers approached and offered his hand.

"Yes," the bartender replied and gave the officer a hearty handshake. "The name on the birth certificate is Asmodeus, but the average bar patron finds it hard to pronounce. You can call me Snake."

"Your mother must have had a sense of humor."

Snake pulled a box out from under the bar, opened it and started rolling a joint right there in front of the cops. They watched him do it and just smiled. How the fuck did he get away with it?

"My father. He named me. Don't have much of a relationship. In fact, I haven't spoken to him in years." He laughed and lit the damn joint, took a long drag while the cops laughed with him.

The satanic references were way too lame to be funny. But they laughed. Did he own them? Was he some bigwig gangster dude with cops on his payroll?

"I want to make you aware there was a planned hit on an elderly man in a nearby neighborhood. Gang initiation of some sort. An anonymous caller tipped us off, and we would love to talk with him further. Since the call was made from one of those prepaid, disposable cell phones, all we know is that it came from this general area."

"If I see or hear anything, I'll let you know." Snake took another drag on the joint.

The other officer looked in my direction, as if looking through me, but taking way too much interest. I turned away, thought it might make me more suspect and stared down at my boots instead.

The initial officer handed Snake one of his cards. "Please feel free to call us anytime."

"How did you do that?" I couldn't help but laugh once the officers had left. The bartender impressed me. Just did whatever the hell he wanted and answered to nobody. Not even the cops.

"So you're the tipster they're looking for?"

"Oh no!"

"Sure you don't want to confess. I heard it's good for the soul."

"I didn't do a damn thing! How did you get away with rolling drugs right there in front of a couple of cops?"

"I have a special way with certain people." He shrugged.

"Certain people?"

"Those who ain't choirboys, son."

"But they're police officers? The good guys?"

"The baddest boys start off as angels." He shrugged, finished up his joint and snuffed it out.

Another waitress came out of the back kitchen area. "Boss!"

"I know," he growled, then turned to me. "Kid, you are getting to be more trouble than you're worth. Come with me. We are going to hang out in my office while I finish up some paperwork."

"I'm not going anywhere with you." He was hot. Big, badass, cock-hardening hot, but something wasn't quite right. Every cell of my body told me not to follow him down those stairs. I'm not the stupid horror-movie kid that goes into the dark knowing I'll get killed.

"Okay. Be that way. The boys interested in that informant are three steps away from the front door. You can hang out with them."

Like I said, I'm not stupid, but I wanted to live. I followed Snake down the stairs.

He sat down behind a big cherrywood desk, opened a bottom drawer and pulled out a bottle of whisky, drank a swig straight from the bottle. "You are not the one I wanted to snag tonight."

I shrugged, standing my ground on the opposite side of his desk. "So sorry to disappoint."

"I'm not disappointed." Snake smiled and patted the seat next to him. "Come. Sit. Let's get to know each other."

He frightened me. I couldn't lie about that. But something in his eyes made me think he was lonely, sad. I understood that completely. I wore those same boots. And he was everything I had fantasized about since I was old enough to fantasize, a big, powerful man who both scared and aroused me. Snake, in his hard-mannered, soft-spoken way, was a wet dream come true.

"Come on, Austin. I don't bite until you beg for it. You know you want to."

Snake, with his curly blond hair, warm gold eyes and the heart-shaped face of an angel with a hint of rough five o'clock shadow tracing his jaw tempted me like I'd never been tempted before. He smiled, his big, plush pink lips framing shiny white teeth. I joined him in the black leather chair next to his and when my bottom made contact with the seat, his hand slid up my thigh to an inch before the tip of my cock.

"Such a beautiful boy." Snake traced the line of my jaw with his thumb. "I remember being so young, so idealistic, so energetic."

"You don't look that old."

"I'm not. Things just get a little monotonous at times. Makes you feel old, you know what I mean?"

"Yes." I did. My twin brother was six minutes younger than me, but taking care of him, cleaning up after him, time after time, made me feel like the older brother and I wanted to break away, too. I was so tired of being the good brother all the time. Just once...

Snake leaned in and kissed me, pressing his soft lips against mine. He tasted like whisky, warm liquor intoxicating me. His tongue tapped against my lips, like asking permission, and I parted them in reply, invited him inside my mouth. His kiss deepened, his tongue hard and strong, teasing and tempting mine. His hands braided in my hair and pulled me closer, making me take even more. Snake's mouth overwhelmed me, I couldn't breathe and it didn't matter.

"Such a good boy," he whispered into the line of my chin, and pressed kisses down the length of my throat. In the little pool of skin at the base, he licked and nibbled, sucked it in. I knew he was leaving a hickey, best bruise I'd ever been given. "Such a good, good boy. I'm going to have so much fun making you mine."

He leaned back into his chair and pulled the tie from his throat, continued to hold it in his hand. I moved to his lap, straddled his legs between mine and slowly unbuttoned his shirt. I pulled it down his arms and smiled along with his smile when it caught at his wrists. Instead of unbuttoning the button at each wrist, I yanked hard and heard them pop, both bits of plastic hitting the ground with little thuds. It pleased him, I could tell.

I kissed his mouth then the tip of his chin while rubbing his hardening nipples with the pad of my thumb. Feeling them respond to my touch made me hard, so hard my erection was finding little room to breath in the denim cave of my jeans. It would have to be let out very soon. But I wanted to show Snake I had skills. I could be just as badass sexy as he was.

I kissed and licked down the hard muscle of his abdomen as he pulled his belt free of the buckle and opened his pants. He spoke commando. With the fly open, nothing kept his dark pink erection from pushing its way up to his belly button. He moved underneath me, and it made his cock tap the little patch of hair on his belly.

"You like that?" he asked.

"Oh yeah."

"Why don't you be a good boy and show me how much you like it?"

I pressed his cock into his stomach and leaned in to lick his balls. The hair surrounding his jewels tickled my nose, and

I loved it. I laved them both up and the underside length of his cock until he moaned and pressed against my mouth. His hands went into my hair again, and he pushed down. "Suck it, damn it!"

I sucked the little dent just below the head of his cock, hard like I planned to leave a hickey. A pearl of come rose to the surface and I tasted it, then took the whole head in my mouth and sucked, coming back up with a loud pop sound. The next dip went deeper and the next, deeper.

Snake wasn't getting what he wanted and pushed my head down hard, going past my normal stopping point and making me gag. "Take it down. All the way."

I tried coming back up but made very little distance before he drove me back down. I felt him go all the way into my throat just like I'd read about in porno mags. Heard it was possible, but I never thought I could do it. But I was doing it, enjoying both the way it felt taking all of him and the way he displayed his pleasure, groaning and face-fucking me.

A loud crash on the floor above us startled me and made me lift my head from his groin. Another soon followed, vibrating the roof above.

"What was that?" I heard some shouting and groans of pain. One of the screams sounded like Ryan.

"Nothing to worry about, Austin. The handful of thug wannabes upstairs weren't prepared for three of my best girls. That's all."

I thought about Ryan, my twin brother, and the gang he called friends. Some of which were probably upstairs now, and they were a lot bigger than any of the waitresses at the bar. I didn't know what I'd be able to do, but I wasn't raised to leave the weaker sex in possible distress. "Maybe we should go up there and check on things."

"I said don't worry about it." He kissed me again, claiming me with his mouth. "If there was anything they couldn't handle, you'd see one of them come running down the stairs screaming, 'Boss!' Come on. It's time for you get naked. I feel some serious muscle under that shirt. Let's see it."

Under his hard gaze and gentle caressing encouragements, in a little time I relented, shrugging myself out of my jacket and pulling the old t-shirt over my head. He leaned back, observed and twisted the tie he still held in his hand, as I kneeled on the floor at his feet and shucked off the boots, undid my jeans and pulled them to my knees.

"Stop right there," Snake commanded.

He lowered to his knees beside me and looked me up and down. I was trapped on my knees, nothing covering my body but the pair of jeans and plain white boxers bunched up between my knees and ankles, pinning me in place. I felt almost helpless, like the beginning of the initiation ritual earlier I'd so obviously failed.

Ryan was the real bad boy, not me. We started out the same, identical twins, but somewhere along the way he made it into the wrong crowd. Started with drug arrests, doing and selling, then moved to robbery when our parents cut him off money-wise. My attempts at shocking consisted of an alcohol-inspired tattoo on my eighteenth birthday and choosing my crushes from the football team instead of the cheerleading squad. Shocking enough in most households, but compared to my brother, it wasn't shit!

Snake pressed his chest against mine and tried to tie my hands behind my back at my wrists.

"No," I whispered.

"Come on, baby. It's really hot. You'll love it. Trust me."

The gang tried to tie me up, and I refused. Took out a few

teeth from the fool with the rope, and my brother had to break it up before I got my ass killed. I wanted to reunite, find closeness with my twin again and, at the time, thought it was the only method.

Snake kissed my cheek. "Have you ever had your cock sucked while you were completely helpless? Couldn't get away no matter how hard you tried? Able to do nothing but come? It'll be the best, most exciting ride of your life."

I wanted fierce. I wanted exciting. And there was something in his strength, the way he carried himself, did what he wanted and answered to no one. He didn't have to yell, scream, throw his weight around or draw a single weapon. His kind of badass just spoke and things happened. I wanted him to fuck me. I wanted to live like I'd never lived before. I wanted to find that connection to my brother's world. Snake was a better answer than joining that damn gang. I moved my wrists, one over the other, and let him tie them together.

Tonight I was supposed to participate in an initiation, talked into it by Ryan. The plan after I wouldn't allow being bound and hazed? Home robbery and roughing up of an elderly man who kept to himself. An old, disabled Marine living in a small house at the end of a cul-de-sac. The kind of guy that inspired kids to tell scary stories about him when wandering through his yard.

When I heard his name, I gasped out. No! When I told Dad I was gay, the Marine was the one who let me hide out in his house, drink a soda, play a few hands of cards and talk until things cooled down and I felt able go home. He listened to me, was a friend when I needed one the most and I could never betray that trust. Yeah, I called the cops. I tried to grab my brother and run, but instead Ryan jerked me by the arm and screamed, "You betrayed us, you fuck! You screwed up everything!"

My eyes met Snake's. I wanted to cry. I longed to be under his protection, fucked until all the bad things in my head went away.

"Looks like you've lost your erection, baby. Your thoughts just wouldn't let you keep it up. Don't worry. I can get it back for you."

I started remembering stuff I didn't know I had forgotten. Snake helped me lie on my side and lowered his head, took me in his mouth. I didn't think my hard-on was going to come back but his mouth and tongue moved over my cock and I felt heat again, a warm flood of sensation in his sucking motions that made me gasp out loud. Nothing had ever felt so good as my cock down his throat. I wanted to put my hands on his head, thrust into his mouth, but I was helpless. I could only absorb the pleasure he gave me.

He rose up from my new erection, fondled my balls and said, "Are you going to be a good boy and let me have that ass?"

I nodded. Snake maneuvered me into position, pressing my cheek into the floor with my ass in the air, my hands still tied behind me. He opened a drawer and removed condoms and lube, suited up his dick and drenched it and my hole in KY. He gripped the bindings at my wrist with one hand while the fingers of the other tested my sphincter. One finger moved to two, and with a resounding pop on my ass with his palm he declared, "My beautiful, sweet angel, you are so ready for a good fucking."

He moved behind me, traced the outline of my tattoo with his finger, ground his testicles into my butt. He used his cock to trace the line of my crack, and inserted it. It hurt. It felt amazing. He was full and heavy and rode me hard, using the tie at my wrist like a harness. "Beg for it, angel. Tell me how bad you want it."

"Please. Fuck me, Snake. Fuck me hard. Come all up in my ass. I want it so bad."

"Tell me you want to be mine."

"I want to be yours, Snake. All yours."

He came with a fierce growl and lay down against the length of my back, pressing kisses into my sweaty spine. After a few breaths, he rose just enough to untie my wrists and put my hand on my cock. "Jerk off like you've just been fucked in the ass."

I did it with his weight over me and the sensation of his cock still stuffed between my asscheeks, filling me to the point of explosion. He told me about all the dirty things he wanted to do to me and where, and I came in a fast gush, all over my stomach and the floor.

It felt like a dream. A hot, sweaty, beyond reality dream.

His phone rang, and he rose up to hit the speaker.

"Boss, some guardians came for the kid. Wanted to take him home, but I said I hadn't seen him. Do you want me to call them back?"

"No!" he replied quickly and hung up.

"What's that about?"

"Like I said, you're not the one I wanted tonight." He sighed. "But you're so pleasing, so refreshing, I want to keep you anyway."

"I don't understand."

"I came for Ryan Gregory. Robbery, rape, murder. Same old, same old. You're just a good Catholic schoolboy, nothing more than a few shades gay. I would normally never come in contact with someone as pure and sweet as you, but you died, and of your own free will, showed up at my doorstep."

Dead? I couldn't breathe. Had I been breathing to begin with? I pressed my hand to my chest and tried to lift up out of his embrace. The pieces were falling into place. Snake. Asmodeus. "Oh my god!"

"No, baby boy. Too late for that. Like I said, you're a gift I wasn't expecting, but I'll cherish you all the more. I'll keep you up high in my chain of command. Personally teach you."

"What do you mean?"

"Your junked-out brother hunted you down like a dog and personally put a bullet in your head to show off to his friends and save his own ass. They tossed your corpse in a dumpster out back. I can show you the remains if you're that desperate to see. The cops probably won't find it for another couple of hours."

"Where's Ryan? I need to talk to him." I struggled to get up and run, not caring that I was naked, but he lifted his hand. The doorknob jerked out of mine and the door slammed shut again.

"I love you so much, Austin. I had my girls put some extra hard in the ass-kicking Ryan and his buddies received upstairs. Sure, I'll take you to see them now, but I must warn you. They look a whole lot worse than what's left of your mortal remains. I think it would be more fun for you to watch them in the pit I have saved especially for their type. Just give Satrinah a moment to find a good place to stash the bodies and get their souls stored."

He came up behind me and wrapped one of his arms around my hip, petted my hair and kissed me softly on the forehead. "My treasure. I didn't mean to scare you. You and your brother, like many twins, switched identities all the time. You were impossible to tell apart, but only one Gregory brother has a tattoo." He kissed my cheek. "I'm a little soul blind and can't tell the difference between the living and the dead until a soul has been separated from its body for a full day or so. I didn't know which brother I had until you told me about your little owl."

"But I can't go to hell. I haven't done anything wrong."

"Doesn't matter, angel. So much like me. I want to possess you over and over again. You came to me and in this corner, I make the rules."

# STRENGTH

## P. L. Ripley

Max saw him standing in front of Kelly's Drugstore, smoking cigarettes, leaning against the wall and looking pissed. He wore black jeans and a sleeveless shirt that showed off his skinny, tattoo-covered arms. The jeans looked dirty and well worn, with frayed cuffs and patches rubbed to near white at the groin and knees. A very impressive lump pushed the material out at the crotch.

The tattoos stretched from his shoulders to wrists. Fat gauges impaled his ears, stretching the lobes to twice their normal length. He had short, spiky red hair that came to points as sharp as needles. When someone walked by him, he would scowl and bark out a little grunt. Max wondered if the guy was all there or not.

"What's the deal with that guy?" Max asked Marlene, the assistant manager of the Coffee Hutch where he was working for the summer. High school had just ended, and he was trying to decide what to do with the rest of his life: go to college or try to climb some sort of financial ladder without it.

"Oh, gross, him," she said, looking out the window.

"You know him?"

"No, but I know his girlfriend, Cheryl. She works at Kelly's. He's been walking her to work and back home for a few days. He thinks she's cheating on him. He's keeping an eye on her."

"Is she? Cheating on him, I mean?" he asked.

"Probably. Look at him."

Max was looking at him, and he wouldn't cheat on him. Max had always loved the rough guys, the punks, the bikers, the bad boys. When he was in high school, now only a few months in his past, he was out, not by choice but because someone found out he was dating another boy and spread the word. The other boys, the jocks, the hoods, looked at him differently after that. He looked at himself differently as well. It was their assumption that gay equals effeminate and effeminate equals weak. Their thoughts rubbed off on him, and he saw himself as less strong. He didn't play sports, smoke or fight. He did none of the things that people see as manly, so they were probably right, he thought. That was why he loved the ruffians. He saw toughness in them he didn't see in himself.

When his break came he told Marlene he was going out for lunch. "Make sure you punch out," she said, and he sailed out to the back room. He removed the sticky apron they made him wear and tossed the Coffee Hutch hat into his locker and walked across the street to the drug store.

He passed by Tattoo Boy and gave him a smile and nod. "How's it going?" he asked.

Tattoo grunted a reply. Max went in the store, bought a pack of Marlboro's, wondering if the chunky blonde girl behind the counter was the infamous girlfriend, and walked back out into the warm August afternoon air. He opened the pack, shoved a cigarette in his mouth and went through a charade of searching for a lighter. He had never smoked a cigarette before, but this was the only way he could think to strike up a conversation with a boy who was currently making him hard.

Tattoo Boy watched his little dance. Max turned to him. "You got a light I can bum?" he asked.

Tattoo game him a half-mouth smirk, exposing a broken front tooth, and dug a lighter from his pocket. It was a Zippo and an expensive one by the looks. He flipped the cover open on his leg, flicked the little wheel and held it before him. Max leaned in until their heads nearly touched and lit the Marlboro. Waves of old sweat stink rolled off Tattoo. Max tried not to inhale on the cigarette, but did anyway. The smoke felt like hot ashes going into his lungs. He coughed until he nearly vomited, spoiling the cool image he was trying to put up for the other boy. "Thanks, man," Max said.

"No problem," he replied, chuckling under his breath. His voice was heavy and deep. It seemed to roll up from the center of his chest. It was a sexy voice. "You sure you want to smoke that?"

"Ugh, I quit a while ago, probably should keep it that way," Max replied, then introduced himself, stretching out a hand.

Tattoo stared at it a second then slowly, almost cautiously took it in his own hand. Max felt a slight tingle pass between them. A little charge of electricity. "Russell...Russ actually," he said, deciding Max was harmless. He fell back against the wall.

"So, I see you've been out here all morning," Max said. "You waiting for someone?"

"What's it to you?" he grumbled, pushing himself away from the wall to stand at his full height of five foot eight. This was nothing compared to Max's six foot stance, but Max knew size isn't everything. Russ had a wiry toughness to him, a hard sure strength that came from physical activity like fighting.

"Nothing. It's nothing to me. Just wondering is all," Max nearly whimpered, bowing his head before the alpha male.

"Sorry," he said. "My girlfriend works in there," he replied, cocking his thumb at the store behind them.

"Oh yeah. Which one is she?" Max asked, glancing through the window like he actually cared who it was.

"The blonde," he said, looking a little upset they were talking about her.

"Oh yeah, she's cute." She wasn't, but he played along.

He glared at Max, his fists pumping in on themselves. Heavy muscle cords rose and fell in his forearms, making the tattoo of the grim reaper on his left arm dance. Max looked down again, giving the subservient stance that seemed to calm him down. "She's a whore," Russ said.

"Why do you say that?"

"She fucks anything with a swinging dick."

"She's cheating on you?" Max asked.

"I think she is. No, let me rephrase that. I know she is."

"She's an idiot then."

He looked at Max quizzically then replayed that broken-toothed smirk. "Why you say that?"

Max stared at him a moment while he stared back with that sexy grin, his hands balled into fists and flexing again. "I'd never cheat on you," Max finally choked out, preparing himself for the punch in the face he knew was coming.

Instead of hitting him though, Russ stepped up to him, their faces even closer now than when he had lit Max's cigarette. "You couldn't handle what I got," he said, and followed it up with, "boy."

Max could smell the strong body odor from him again and

was a little disgusted with himself to discover he was getting hard from it. He swallowed, deeply, and inhaled the other man's heady stink. His mouth felt like sandpaper. What he said next could either make him a friend or get his ass kicked right here on the sidewalk in front of the Coffee Hutch. Max looked into his eyes, his beautiful blue-gray eyes, and said, "Maybe not, but it would be fun trying."

Russ took a quick step back, fists pumping in on themselves like he was gaining strength from it, getting stronger, getting ready to strike. Then his face split in half with a huge smile. He let out a little laugh, a laugh that was mostly joy and just a tiny bit of menace. "You're weird," he said and leaned back against the drugstore wall again, his pierced left eyebrow raised in curiosity.

Max exhaled in relief. He hadn't struck him, but that didn't mean he was interested either. Russ shoved his hands in his jeans pockets, and to Max's eyes the ample crotch seemed a bit more ample. Perhaps it was just his imagination. It was possible Russ had gotten a little exited by the comments, but it still meant nothing. Max was always flattered when a girl came on to him; it didn't mean he would do anything with her, but yes, it did turn him on a little that someone found him attractive. Even if he wasn't attracted to them.

"I gotta go back to work. Thanks for the light," Max said, and quickly made his way back to the Coffee Hutch.

When his shift was over Max bought two coffees and walked back to Kelly's Drugstore. Russ was still out there, still waiting for his cheating girlfriend to get out of work. Max handed him one of the steaming cups. "What's this for?" Russ asked, an eyebrow arched.

"You've been out here all day. Figured you might be thirsty."

"Look," Russ spat, the newly rising fury turning his face

red, "if you're up to something I…"

Max cut him off. "I'm not up to something. You looked like you could use something to drink, that's all. If you don't want it I'll drink it."

Russ gave a sheepish look. He was the one to look to the ground this time. "I'm…I'm sorry, man. Thanks for the coffee."

"You're welcome."

The two stood side by side, sipping the coffees, the warm summer day fading to warm summer evening. Russ smoked cigarette after cigarette until he crumpled the empty pack and tossed it to the ground. "Outta smokes," he said.

Max dug the pack of Marlboro's he had bought earlier. "Take these," he said. "I decided to stay off them."

"Thanks again, man," Russ said and pulled one out. He looked at Max curiously, raising that pierced eyebrow again, which got the blood churning through Max's crotch.

"I'm surprised they haven't told you to leave yet. I mean, most places wouldn't want someone loitering around all day," Max said.

"I know the owner," Russ replied. It was the only explanation needed apparently.

Finally Cheryl stepped out of the store and Russ pushed himself from the wall. The heavy blonde wrapped an arm around Russ and started pulling him down the sidewalk. Russ turned to Max. "Thanks for the coffee and smokes."

"No problem," Max replied. "See you around."

"Yeah, I hope I do."

As the couple walked away, arms around each other, Max heard Cheryl ask, "Who was that faggot?"

Russ pulled his arm away from her. "Shut the fuck up, you dumb bitch."

Max crossed the street to the parking lot where his old Chevy sat, got in, and drove home.

The next few days Max brought Russ coffee and hung out with him until his break would end. After work he would sit in his car, backed into the middle spot in the lot behind the Coffee Hutch and drink even more coffee. From this vantage he could look out the alley and see Russ leaning against the drugstore wall. If the light was right Russ could see him too.

"This is stupid," he mumbled to himself. The two were becoming friendly, but it was obvious Russ wasn't interested. Max had thrown several leading comments but Russ hadn't bitten on any of them. If he was curious, he would have thrown something back, right?

Max would complement him and Russ would simply smile that broken-toothed smile, cock the pierced eyebrow, and then Max would get a hard-on and they would move on to another subject.

Then one day, as the warm September afternoons became cool October evenings, Russ and Cheryl exploded into a fight in front of the drugstore. Max was in his car, as usual, and watched the entire event.

Cheryl came out of the store when her shift ended and had some sort of bug up her ass. She immediately began screaming at Russ for no reason that Max could discern. Russ just stood, stunned by her outburst until she slapped his face and began punching him in the arms and chest. He pushed her away. She came back with a slap to his face then marched off. He tried to follow her but she spun on him, stuck a middle finger, with a heavily lacquered fingernail, in the air and said something that stopped Russ where he was, then marched off.

Max sat, stunned. He had been holding his breath through the entire confrontation and once it was over let his breath out with a deep *Humph*.

Russ walked back to the drugstore. His head was down, that old humbled look again, and he stopped when he arrived at the spot where he had spent the last week. He looked up, right at Max in his car. He puffed himself up again, and marched down the alley, coming right at Max.

Max was just about to get out, to ask if he was okay, when Russ tore open the door, grabbed Max by the shirt and pulled him out. He slammed him against the side of the car, driving the door handle in Max's back. Pain shot down his legs.

"What the fuck?" Max cried out, as Russ pulled his arm back, fist hovering before his face.

Max could try to fight him, but there was no point. Even if he could get in a few swings, Russ could pummel him in seconds. He closed his eyes and waited for the inevitable, for the strike that never came. Instead of the pain of his cheekbone shattering he felt pressure on his lips. He opened his eyes as Russ leaned back.

What just happened, he wondered. It felt like a kiss but...then Russ moved in again pressed his lips against Max's, this time harder, much harder. Their teeth ground together. Max opened his mouth and let his tongue fall against Russ's. Max kissed him back with all the ferocity Russ gave him. He pulled Russ close and could feel the other boy's hardening cock press against his leg.

Max looked into Russ's eyes, those beautiful blue-gray pools, and saw anger in them. Anger, rage and a heavy dose of fear.

Max opened his mouth to say something, anything, but Russ stopped him.

"Don't," was all he said, then began tugging at Max's belt. He opened Max's pants and shoved them around his ankles, then dropped to his knees. If anyone happened to look down the alley they would see them, but Max didn't care and suspected Russ didn't either.

Max moaned as his cock slid into Russ's mouth and he shuddered with the hot, moist wonder of it. He felt the roving tongue slide up and down the shaft while the head was pulled on with vacuum-like suction. The tongue slid along the underside, over the top, and then tickled the crown. Warm saliva ran down to Max's balls, collecting in the thick hair on his scrotum.

Max set his hands on Russ's head, running his fingers through the spiky, heavily gelled locks of flaming hair. Russ reached up and knocked his hands away. Pulling his mouth from Max he looked up. "Don't touch me," was all he said and went back to work. When he slid that broken tooth the length of Max's dick and scraped it along the head, Max nearly clawed his way backward over the roof of the car. It was the most intensely painful pleasure he had known up to that point.

"Oh Jesus!" Max groaned.

Russ smiled around the dick, pulling it even harder and faster into his face.

It had been a long time since Max had been with anyone and it didn't take any time at all before his balls pulled up into his body and the impending orgasm churned away inside, ready to strike out. Russ must have felt it too—the extraordinary hardening of Max's cock, the short quick breaths, the quick jerks of his hips—and he pulled off him before he blew. "Not yet," he muttered, and slid Max from the car door, opened it and shoved him inside.

Max fell on the seat in a tumble, his pants still around his ankles, trapping his legs together. Russ reached in, shucked Max's shoes from his feet and tore at his pants. He dropped them onto the car floor, the change in the jeans pockets spilling everywhere. He tore his own clothes off and slid in on top of Max, naked, with an erection already dripping with excitement.

Max noticed the tattoos didn't end with his arms. There

were patterns and pictures and words running down his side, over his back and chest and even 9 INCHES stenciled along his dick. Both of his nipples were pierced and a heavy ring hung from the urethra on his cock, pushing the heavy sweater of foreskin from the head.

Russ reached down, removed the Prince Albert and shoved his cock in Max's face. It smelled of sweat and a slight tinge of piss. Max pulled it into his mouth anyway. He had been admiring Russ and what might be lurking in those pants for so long he couldn't let this moment go without recognition, without fulfilling what he surely wanted, what he needed.

"Oh fuck," Russ groaned and slid himself deeper into Max's throat. Max pulled him in, feeding on every inch given to him. He ran his hands up Russ's body, feeling the hard muscles lying just beneath the wiry frame of his hips, back and chest.

Russ pulled Max's head up, and held it while he thrust in and out of his mouth.

Max could feel it tear at his larynx, push down toward his lungs. He couldn't breathe, couldn't swallow. Russ's strong arms wouldn't release him and Max wasn't sure if he wanted him to. He thought for a moment he was going to be strangled to death with this beautiful cock. Just as panic began to settle in, Russ released him and Max inhaled a very welcome breath, yet oddly enough felt a moment of disappointment. His throat felt empty, lonely and unloved.

Russ pulled all the way out, bent down and kissed Max again. "I'm going to fuck you," he said, and spun Max over in the seat.

Fear screamed through Max's brain. He had never been fucked before, never had a finger, let alone a cock as large as this, in there.

"Please," Max groaned, "I've never..."

"I don't care," he whispered, giving Max's ear a slight bite. Max heard him spit onto his cock and felt the hard pressure of the head pushing against his hole. He tensed and Russ tried to ease him by rubbing his back and ass. "Just relax. It will hurt less."

Max tried but when the first few inches slid in he thought he was being torn in half. He bit the seat and screamed into the foam. Russ pumped his hips, back and forth, back and forth, getting a good momentum up, but keeping most of himself out of Max.

The pain dulled and lying just beneath it was a hint of pleasure. Soon, the pleasure overtook the pain and Max began to understand the attraction of this. He reached back and felt only about four inches, less than half of what Russ had to offer, sliding in and out between his asscheeks. Russ didn't want to hurt him, not seriously at least.

But Max wanted more of him. He asked him to go all the way in, but he wouldn't. "This is enough," he said, and grunted as he kept pumping at the hole, regulating how much he fed in. Max wanted more, and he was going to get it. When Russ pushed in Max suddenly lifted his hips from the seat and pushed back. The final five inches rammed into him and he nearly bucked Russ off him. The pain was even more intense than when he had first been entered.

Russ yelped and tried to pull away, but Max wouldn't let him. It hurt like a son-of-a-bitch, but he wanted him, all of him, and he was going to get it. Whether Russ wanted to give it or not.

Russ got the hint and pushed him back down and slammed into him again, his heavy balls slapping Max's ass as he fed his cock to him. He pulled almost all the way out, just the head trapped in the heavy ring of Max's ass, then pushed back in until his pubic bone smashed against the other boy's asscheeks.

He repeated this again and again. Max was going mad; it felt so good, so filling.

Max lifted his hips and Russ reached down and grabbed his cock. It stood like iron in his fist. He pumped it, stroked it, teased the head with his fingertips and tugged on the heavy, hairy nuts, all the while plowing into him with all the fierceness of a madman.

Max's balls began to tighten just as they had when he was getting sucked, and he hoped Russ would let him come this time.

Russ synchronized his pumps on Max's cock with the thrusts at his ass, and before Max could warn him he shot onto the car seat. His hole tightened, clamping down on the fat meat inside him. Russ grunted from the pressure then banged into him a few more times before his screams filled the car and he came deep inside Max.

He dropped down onto Max, his sweat-glistening body sticky, his breath hot and laced with cigarette aftereffects. Russ lay on Max's back, panting while his cock shrunk and finally plopped out of Max's ass.

Max turned his head, found Russ's mouth and kissed him. Russ pulled away and slid out of the car. He was half-dressed when Max rolled over and began slipping his own pants on.

"I'm not queer you know," Russ said. "I don't care what that bitch says." He lit a cigarette and pushed blue smoke from his mouth. Max put his shirt on and stood beside him, not saying anything.

"I'm not queer."

"Okay," Max replied, "does this mean we can't do this again?"

"Cheryl is pregnant," he said. "This was hot, real hot but..." he looked over at Max, and took his hand. Max's smooth unblemished skin lay covered by Russ's star-tattooed hand. "You are hot, but Cheryl can't find out. My kid isn't even born yet, and she's already threatening to take him away from me."

"And that means…"

"That means we can do this, but we have to be real careful. You can't hang out with me anymore. We will have to meet secretly. If she finds out…shit."

Max hadn't been in the closet since before high school. It was difficult outside, but more difficult in. Even to fool around with someone as hot as Russ he wouldn't go back in. He had decided a long time ago to live his life his way and to hell with what other people thought.

He had thought Russ was tough, but Russ was taking the easy way. He would have his wife and kids and live the illusion of "normal" while Max would be out there fighting the good fight. It didn't mean that Russ didn't want a wife and kids, but he wanted a man as well and he chose the safest route. The secret route.

Max realized then that *he* was the tough one. He might not play sports or smoke or fight, but he was stronger than Russ would ever be. He would never allow anyone to tell him how he should be.

He still loved the tough guys, and always would; the tattoo punks, the leather men, the biker hogs, but if they wanted to be with him they had to be as tough as he was.

# DIRTY LIAR

## Fox Lee

I love my job, I do. That said, there are times when it gets under my skin like a rash, and makes me wonder why I didn't listen to my mother and become an accountant. An accountant can work regular hours and go home every night secure that he'll be sleeping in his own bed. As a private detective in Tokyo, one of the most expensive cities in the world, my life is a cycle of feast and famine.

Then again, it was better than unemployment. My first case was for an ex-boyfriend, the one who left me for an arranged marriage when his parents made it clear that it was either that or kiss his trust fund good-bye. Not a year after the wedding, he asked me to find out if she was cheating on him. At the time I was face-to-face with eviction and eventual starvation, so I was willing to swallow my pride and forget what a sackless asshole he was. Within two days I had everything he needed. The wife was fucking his father, who arranged the whole marriage so that he could keep her as his mistress.

As fucked up as the case was, it kick-started my career. Word of mouth spread, and I became Japan's go-to guy for cuckolded men. Given that I was openly gay, my clients didn't worry that I would take liberties with a promiscuous wife or lover. My friends even gave me a new title: Atsuto Honda, Slut Hunter. My cases were usually pretty straightforward, no pun intended. All I had to do was tail the woman long enough to catch her doing the wrong thing. Occasionally, I had to go undercover. My last job, for example, was to investigate a wife whose husband suspected her of sleeping with her boss.

Since the affair was in the workplace, I had to get a job at her company and blend in. That meant a new suit, no more jewelry, and a conservative haircut. Before that I had a goatee, long hair and pierced ears. The earrings were easy enough to put back in, but the haircut stung. I knew it would be months before I looked like myself again. After the case was over, and I proved the wife was riding her boss like he was an amusement park ride, I needed to lick my wounds so I collected my money and headed south to a *ryokan,* an old-style Japanese inn. Hell, if I was going to look like an upstanding citizen I was going to take advantage of it.

It was a bit of an extravagance. The *ryokan* was far from cheap, and I knew the bill would come around to bite me in the ass. Even so, the first day alone made it worth the money. Had I been a straight man, I could have definitely gotten myself into trouble. The women who brought me my meals and tended to my room were beautiful. Of course, I was more interested in the food. I wouldn't say it was as good as sex, but damn it came close. Between that, the rural scenery and the *ryokan's* hot spring public bath, I was ready to turn to jelly.

The only thing the inn was missing was eye candy. All the other men were too old for my taste, or simply not my type. I didn't really mind: I came there to unwind, not get laid. Plus my appearance had me feeling self-conscious. I finally looked like the accountant my mother dreamed of, and it drove me crazy. It was too clean cut. Even if I had been back in Tokyo, I doubted I would have attracted the kind of man I was looking for.

The day before I was scheduled to leave, I took my last trip to the hot bath. It was a gorgeous setup: lots of room to soak, and a window that overlooked the koi pond in the inn's garden. There were already eight people in the bath, some talking politely with each other while others drifted off into their own thoughts. Serenity at its finest; I knew I would be sad to say good-bye. The heat of the water had begun to permeate my muscles nicely, when the room went dead quiet. I looked up to see three men standing at the far side of the bath. Two were in dark suits and wore sunglasses.

The third man was the one that caught my interest. Despite being on the short side, his presence was intense. He scanned the room, his dark eyes impassive. It wasn't uncommon for hot springs to refuse guests with tattoos. Clearly this *ryokan* didn't care, or else didn't dare argue with their new guest. His chest and arms were covered.

I suddenly noticed that everyone else was leaving. They looked scared, as if sure that one misstep was all it would take to end up at the bottom of the koi pond outside. I was about to follow, when the man's gaze locked on me.

"You stay."

He gestured to men behind him, who bowed and left the room. I could tell that this was not a man I wanted to fuck with. He was the real-life version of the men I usually went after, the ones that looked like bad boys on the surface but were sweet underneath. Maybe I was a coward, but at the end of the day I preferred the illusion of danger to the real thing. At the moment, however, I wasn't being given the choice. The man with the tattoos watched closely as I got back into the water, and the look in his eyes was hardly subtle.

Once I was seated, he slowly entered the bath, and crossed over to my side. His body was compact, tight muscles wrapped in smooth tan flesh. My cock twitched under the water. Unlike my brain, it had little regard for my well-being. The primal part of my brain liked what it saw and wanted to play.

"You look like a nice boy," the man said. "You come here with a pretty little girlfriend?"

"No. No girlfriend," I told him.

"That's okay." He edged closer, until another inch would have pressed our chests together. "You will keep me company."

I swallowed hard, and tried to look every bit the helpless victim. If it came to a fight for my life, I needed the upper hand. The man put his hand on the back of my neck, and lightly drew it down across my collarbone.

"What's your name, pretty boy?" He asked.

"Atsuto."

"You call me Yuuji." He leaned forward, to whisper into my ear. "But only when I am inside you."

Yuuji took my hand and brought it to his cock. Fat and uncut, it swelled at my touch.

"Now," Yuuji said, "make me stiff."

I told myself to be careful. Yuuji clearly thought I was an inexperienced guy, and a straight one at that. Luckily I was so nervous that it was as if I had never touched my own cock before, let alone another man's. Yuuji placed his hand over mine, until I got the pace right. His other hand reached for my nipple. He rubbed softly at first, then gave it a sharp pinch. When I cried out, he smiled.

"Your girlfriends have been too gentle with you."

He pinched again, then moved to the other one. Meanwhile my hand continued to stroke his cock. Unable to display any of the tricks I'd picked up over the years, I kept the moves extremely basic. I'm not saying it was a bad hand job, but I assumed for him the thrill of abusing my naiveté had to be the real turn-on. Yuuji groaned, and released my bruised left nipple. He kissed me roughly, his hips moving in time with his tongue.

My cock screamed for attention. A hand, a mouth, anything to relieve the pressure cooker that had taken up residence in my balls. I kissed Yuuji back timidly, to keep up appearances. He grabbed the back of my hair and pulled my head away.

"I'm sorry," I stammered, terrified that I was about to be beaten within an inch of my life.

"You're a good boy," Yuuji soothed. "Let's see how long you can hold your breath."

I had time to take one big gulp of air, then I was under. My hand was still around Yuuji's cock, which I guided into my mouth as fast as I could. I prayed he was close. As far as I knew, I could only hold my breath for a minute, maybe two. And that was without giving head. My tongue and lips went into overdrive. I sucked and teased Yuuji's shaft, and used my hands to stroke his thighs. After less than a minute, his body tensed and his cock released its load into my mouth.

Yuuji released my hair, and I emerged from the water gasping for breath. The next thing I knew, I was being lifted up by my legs and thrown backward onto the stone floor. Yuuji appeared above me, his face severe.

"Fucking liar," he growled. "Did you just learn to suck dick today?"

He knelt on top of me, a leg on each side of my hips, and held my wrists down. My cock wilted, seemingly aware of how serious the situation was.

"You wanted a pure boy," I said. "Who am I to defy you?"

Yuuji stared at me for a moment, then burst into laughter.

"You want to cover your ass, huh?"

"I don't want to die."

Yuuji sat up and gave me the same smile he did when he heard me cry out in the bath.

"You think I want to kill you?" He asked. "You'd have to piss me off a lot more, or at least be uglier."

He smacked my cheek and called out for someone named Hiroshi. One of the men from before came in, with a small leather satchel.

"This one is sneaky," Yuuji told him. "I need to be careful."

He got off me and stood to the side while Hiroshi knelt between my legs. Hiroshi opened the satchel and removed a small bottle, and a box of condoms. Next, he took out what looked like a doctor's glove. The snap of latex proved I was right. While his boss supervised, Hiroshi lubed up a finger and spread my legs. He teased my asshole, swirling his fingertip around it before slowly inserting the digit.

From the stoic expression on Hiroshi's face, I knew he was simply following orders. It didn't matter to me one way or the other; I was hard again, and I wanted Yuuji to fuck me. Instead he stood there, casually stroking his own cock. Though I had both hands free, I knew better than to use them on myself. If Yuuji wanted me to jerk off, he would tell me.

"Look Hiroshi," he said. "I think the pretty boy is going to pass out if he doesn't come soon."

Hiroshi grunted agreement and added another finger. The tempo increased, and I couldn't stop myself from moaning. Yuuji immediately ordered Hiroshi to stop.

"You don't moan like that for him, pretty boy. Only for me."

Hiroshi made way for his boss, who took my asshole in one rough thrust. Fortunately I was lubed well, and the action brought more pleasure than pain. Yuuji fucked me harder, until the head of my dick beat a frantic rhythm against my stomach. My right hand betrayed me and gripped the dancing member. Yuuji pulled up and flipped me onto my stomach. Both of my hands flew up to protect my face then to brace myself as he resumed his assault from behind.

"Yuuji-san," I begged. "I have to come. Please!"

"When I'm done with you."

He reached around and touched me, too lightly to do any good. I thought I was going to cry. Yuuji tickled my balls next then went back up my shaft. He traced little patterns up and down it, all the while fucking me so hard that I saw spots. Sweat trickled down my ribs and face, and dripped onto the floor. I was panting, bleary eyed and barely able to hold myself steady, when Yuuji came inside me. He roared and dug his fingernails into my hips.

I collapsed onto the floor. My arms shook too badly to masturbate, and I resigned myself to a night of blue balls. Yuuji squeezed my cock and ran his thumb through the pool of precum on the tip.

"The pretty boy did a good job," he told Hiroshi. "Come finish what you started."

My mind was too fuzzy to understand what Yuuji meant, then I felt Hiroshi's mouth on me. It only took seconds for me to come.

"I am staying for the week," Yuuji said, as Hiroshi gathered up his things. "You are staying too."

"No money," I muttered, still dazed.

Yuuji smirked. "Then you don't have to pay."

After he was gone, I eased myself back into the hot spring.

It wasn't particularly sanitary for future bathers, but I needed to ease my aching body. If Yuuji got his way, and I knew he would, I would be spending a lot of time in there. Truth be told, I couldn't wait for the next day.

# BUSTIN'
# OUR BALLS

## Landon Dixon

It was a shitty hotel on the downtown fringe of Philly. There was nothing on the idiot box, less on the streets. So I was holed up in my room amusing myself—my dick in my hand. I was stroking quick and tight, cock hard and glistening with the gun oil I use when the door splintered open and a guy burst inside.

"Freeze, scumbag!" he yelled, leveling a rod at my head.

My hand did freeze on my dick, a scowl on my face. "Jurgens!" I spat it out.

"*Agent* Jurgens to you, Kives." He stepped over the broken wood and right into the room, slammed shut what was left of the door on its busted hinges. The rod stayed steady in his other mitt, .44-caliber black eye staring me down.

"So, you got the bum's rush out of Pittsburgh—rode out on a rail," he crowed, sticking it in my craw, walking up to the lumpy bed and my long, tall cock. "You're becoming small potatoes, Kives. Hardly worth the effort to chase after anymore."

"Like hell," I snarled.

I started pumping heat back into my dick, nice and slow now, putting on a show, stroking all along the turgid length with my gripping paw, swirling blunt fingers over bloated hood real soft. I was bare-ass naked, my own rod sleeping under the pillow that propped up my back against the headboard. My hairy pecs popped, as I dug my hairy balls out from between my muscled legs and squeezed the heavy pair with one hand and stroked my heavy dong with the other.

Jurgens licked his lips, not looking so damn smug and authoritative anymore. He cocked his rod up, giving the warm gaze to my hot genitals. Sure, he had me dead-to-rights, wanted on maybe fifteen statewide warrants and a few national ones. But his sworn duty couldn't stand up to the pulsating height and width of my cock, the sensuous heft and musk of my nuts. I knew the slot machine racket in Philly was over for me, but I wasn't going away without a suck-off send-off.

"You're a hard man to find, Kives," Jurgens gritted. "Harder to take."

The big blond gorilla holstered his rod and unzipped his backup piece, draping his own cock out into the open. It hung down long and wide even semierect, swelling fast. He laced a long-fingered hand around it, lifted and tugged, looming large next to me.

I pumped my cock and twisted my balls, staring at Jurgens's stiffening dong. We were on opposite sides of the law, sure, but he was built big as me, smooth and clean-cut like his profession, cock and balls pink and hairless. I was swarthier, my meat vein-piped. We each carried a load, and a lust.

"Yeah, so you got the drop on me. So what?"

"So this," he said, sinking to his knees alongside me and grabbing onto my cock.

"Fuck!" I grunted, jerking. The man dealt a hot hand.

I planted my mitts on my pecs and mauled the humped pair, fingered the thick olive tips, all the while staring at Jurgens's strong, pale hand shifting up and down my straining pole, feeling it deep in my balls and the back of my skull. The guy knew how to take a man—and torque him but good. His technique was impeccable, pumping me even harder and longer, forging my fucking steel. He dipped his blond head down and slipped his red lips over my cap.

"Fuck! Yeah!" I bellowed, bucking into the guy's moist velvet mouth.

I surged with juice and joy, as Jurgens dropped his head down lower—mouth, lips and tongue—inhaling my cock right to the boiling balls in one heady plunge. He kept me locked down in his craw, sealed tight and beating in the cauldron of his sensual mouth and silky, squeezing throat: a real-life sword swallower. His blues met mine, his nostrils flared for air, flush lips kissed my pubes. He kept right on fisting his own dick as he deep-throated mine.

Muscles quivered and bunched over my burly body. I couldn't take the oral interrogation, the wet-satin pressure on my pulsing pipe was too much for me. I thrust up, knocking Jurgens's head back. He started bobbing his gourd, sucking on my throbbing prong full length and flat out.

I shifted down lower on the bed. His vacuuming mouth never left my cock, his throat happily accommodating all the meat I had to offer. I rasped, "Give *me* some of the good stuff." And he crawled up onto the bed, swinging a leg over my melon, planting his kneecaps on either side. His dong hung down into my lips and I gulped up the beefstick like a starving man.

Jurgens's big, rounded buttocks spasmed in my gripping hands, as I gobbled his swollen shaft deep as he'd taken mine.

His cock plugged my throat and filled my mouth. I rocked my head, sucking on his dick, matching his mouth-pumping motion on my cock. His hips moved like mine, feeding our hunger. I nosed his nuts with each upward gulp.

We hit the right notes, the high notes. His manly groans of delight vibrated all along my mouth-buried cock and through my rippling body. I bucked and blasted ball-batter up against Jurgens's tonsils. His cock spasmed and spray-painted my throat with hot, salty semen.

We jerked and jetted into each other's mouths, in each other's arms, jumping around on the creaking bed until our pipes were drained and we were sucking on spent.

I was out of town a half-hour later.

There was an alley that ran in back of the houses. It was a shitty section of Chi, dilapidated drug dens and boozecans lining the dimly lit streets. There wasn't much light in that alley, either, but I recognized those asscheeks clenching and slamming cock into another man from behind, knew the grunting voice very well.

Jurgens had some punk up against the garage of a house. He was drilling into his chute; the big man's dimpled, glowing buttocks thrusting powerfully and rhythmically. I'd been in the firetrap two doors down, delivering some shine; found the fucking pair in the alley on my way back to my car.

"Keep that rod where I can't see it," I growled, jamming my own iron into Jurgens's back.

He froze in the punk's anus, cheeks quivering. Then he twisted his hard, handsome mug around and scoped my rugged pan. "Kives!" he hissed.

"Yeah, looks like I got the drop on *you* this time, lawman." I pulled the steel mouth of my .45 out of the small of his back.

I jerked my konk at the kid with his hands splayed up against the garage, pants down around his ankles, cute little black ass packed full of Jurgens's huge club. "Interrogating Drop-Down, huh? He tell you anything about me?"

"Plenty," Jurgens gritted, his eyes flashing in the night. "Seems you've muscled in on the illegal, tax-free liquor business in this area, set yourself up quite a string of stills and booze-cans."

Drop-Down squealed, "No, Mr. Kives! I didn't say nuthin' about—"

"Stow it, punk! Everyone knows you got a mouth that can't stay closed. Like you got a pair of pants that can't stay up." I glanced from Drop-Down's frightened, pretty face to Jurgens's grimacing clock. "That's why they call him Drop-Down this end of town, lawman."

"So, what are you going to do, scumbag?"

I grinned, harshly. "Plug you, what else?"

Drop-Down's big brown eyes got a lot bigger.

I stuffed the shooter into my jacket pocket, unbelted and unzipped my pants. Both men watched me, breathlessly, gulping at the sight of the solid length of hose I let loose in that alley. I gripped my dick with one hand and frisked lube out of Jurgens's pocket with the other. Then I greased my dong good and gleaming, busted my cap through the blond's bunched buttocks.

"Yes!" the dirty Fed groaned, thrust deeper into Drop-Down by the force of my hood splitting his ring, plugging into his ass.

I grasped his broad shoulders and plowed inch after inch of bloated, vein-popped shaft into his hot, gripping anus, impaling the guy on my pole like he was already staking out Drop-Down's sweet ass. Both men breathed easy, breathed hard. I thumped up against Jurgens, stretching and stuffing and stoking his chute with my pipe. He drilled into Drop-Down in rhythm.

The night-shaded alley echoed with three-man combined grunts and groans now, the crack of two sets of thighs smacking two sets of buttocks, the squelching of a pair of hard dicks fucking a pair of hot chutes. Sweat beaded my brow, rolled down my armpits. I dug my digits deep into Jurgens's flared traps and rammed his ass with a brutal intensity, feeling every heated plunge to the depth of my prick and my soul. He cocked the kid just as hard and as long and as heavy, pounding Drop-Down almost right through the wall.

"I should turn you in for fucking with a witness!" I rasped in Jurgens's ear, bouncing the big man back and forth on the end of my pumper.

"Yes, but you won't!" he snapped back, blasting Drop-Down's ass with his cock. "Or I'll bust you like I could've for years!"

He had a point. I had a point. We'd been making it for, yeah, years—literally and figuratively.

I fucked Jurgens's ass in a frenzy. He caught the fever pitch, injected it into Drop-Down. The kid clawed at the wood, crying with abandon. He'd been hammered before, lots of times, but never this hard and this fast, by two old pros. He screamed, wildly shaking, going off against the wall.

Jurgens lurched against me, launching a sackful of hot sperm into Drop-Down's jumping black ass. I banged, blazed away, emptying my own rod into the sucking tight tunnel of Jurgens's quivering ass. The three of us spouted off full-bore, jerking together like the cars of a train shunting to a sudden and violent stop.

The lawman and I were both out of town one hour later, headed in separate directions.

* * *

It was outside the jungle room in back of the sleazy strip club
that Jurgens and I butted heads yet again. In fact, we just about
ran face-first into each other, when his boss, Special Agent
Carruthers, ducked into the room after my boss, Lucky Luigi
Calabrese, had gone in a second before. The city was L.A., a
shitty section of town, the time dead of night.

"Slumming?" I jibed at the blond. "Me too."

His plush lips twisted a grin. "Scumbag bodyguard for a
scumbag crime boss? You're nosing rock-bottom, Kives."

"I'm touching it," I countered, looping a big mitt around and
grabbing onto the guy's ass.

He shoved me up against the wall, fists clutching chest hairs.
"I'm on business, jerk-off!"

I kept my hand on his ass, kneading the hard, hilled flesh.
"Yeah, dirty business. Your boss is getting the big payoff from
mine."

"Bullshit! They're talking deal."

I latched my other hand onto his other buttcheek, staring
into Jurgens's stone-set mug. "Yeah, that's what I said. Only the
money's going from my guy to yours. You figure it out."

His blue eyes were ice-cold marbles, his hard body burning
against mine, hot breath scalding my lips. Then suddenly,
savagely, he mashed his mouth into my mouth. Our throbbing
cocks jammed together in the blowtorch heat of our passion.
Fuck our bosses, we had our own private business to tend to!

The wall thumped with the bass of the stripper beat in the
bar, men yelling and hollering. But there were just the two
men in that breathless dark hallway in back, their gorilla arms
wrapped around each other, urgently thumping cocks, excitedly
sucking face, swiping tongue.

Our jackets were off, our shirts torn asunder. I ripped

Jurgens's pants open and down. He returned the erotic favor. We blazed close to naked, muscle-bound, huge cocks pumped.

Then we grappled again, pressing together in a torrid alliance of cock-skin and scrotum, kissing, Frenching, and pumping to our own frenzied beat. Our jobs, our duties were abandoned along with our rods in the forge of our passion, our lust unleashed. We grabbed onto each other's heads and flogged tongues, frotted cocks, wildly, wantonly.

I dove my hands down onto Jurgens's mass-mounded ass, dug my blunt fingertips into the twin-heaped flesh. He grunted, spraying spit into my open mouth. His mitts followed my lead, locking onto my hairy buttocks, squeezing and groping the pair. We ground our cocks up and down, fucking foreskins.

The door popped open. Calabrese and Carruthers stared at us, the high-level lawman slotting a thick envelope into his suit pocket as he gaped. Their dirty business was concluded, but ours had yet to be fully consummated.

"Kives! What the fuck?" Calabrese snarled.

"Agent Jurgens! Desist!" Carruthers chimed in with his paymaster.

But there was no stopping us now, no matter how many crooks gathered to watch. We'd worked ourselves too long and too hard. Our sweaty torsos stuck together, our cocks electra-gliding in flesh tones.

I pulled Jurgens's pucker open with my fingers, plunged into his gaping pink anus with a pair of my digits. He did the same, pouring three fingers of poker into my hole, even deeper. We pumped each other's rectums, as we surged the semen out of our kissing balls and up our rubbing cocks. We exploded together in each other's mouths and arms and cocks and asses, shuddering, grunting, jetting juice in between us in geysering gushes.

Our two bosses went for their rods, maybe disgusted by our

reckless display of manly affection. Maybe turned on and too disgusted with themselves to admit it. Who knew? We knew what to do, though, breaking apart and slamming the men's gun hands down, setting the pair on ice with a couple of straight rights to the jaws.

Then we garbed our steaming physiques, held hands and made tracks for the exit.

We were out of town in fifteen minutes, headed in the same direction, together at last.

# A RIDE ON
# A LEXUS

## Reginald T. Jackson

Lex looked even better than I remembered, and I was glad. Sometimes your mind can play tricks on you and make people seem better in your fantasies than they were in real life. Not this time. He was bangy down and delicious to look at. He stood six feet two with a rock-hard body and tattoos running down his right arm. Dark chocolate complexion, a goatee and thick, juicy, LL Cool J lips. He had on baggy jeans with his boxers showing, a T-shirt that showed off his rock-hard abs and a cap on backward. He could have just stepped off the set of the latest Snoop Dogg or Nelly video.

Slowly he became more and more animated as we talked. Suddenly he moved his bar stool so that he could directly face me, and he slipped my knees between his legs. We talked and talked as I stole a feel of his muscular thighs. Next thing we knew we were the only two people left in the bar. The place was closing and we were being thrown out. I panicked as we walked toward the door. He hadn't asked for my phone number yet, so

I had to find a cute, sexy and subtle way of offering it.

"I'll walk you to the Path train. I can get your number there," Lex said, much to my delight. On the way down the block, I ran into Anthony, who had introduced us earlier that night and was very pleased to see us still together. "Ask him to come home with you," Anthony goaded. "He has tra-a-ade down! Just like you like it," Anthony added, making my heart beat faster.

"What if he says no?" I offered in a pained whine. "I'd turn to dust right there on the spot."

"I know Lex. He likes you. If he didn't want to fuck you he would have dumped you a long time ago. If he's giving you all this attention, he wants to get all up in those guts!" Anthony said, like the voice of reason he usually was.

Once we reached the Path station, I started acting very coy and flirty. I commented on his dark, bedroom eyes and told him how I hated for the evening to end. He said he did also. I took a deep breath, crossed my fingers, closed my eyes and blurted out: "Would you like to come to Jersey with me?"

"I have no problem with that."

Once we were inside my place, I offered him a drink, hoping he'd make a move after a little more alcohol. When I appeared with the very strong drinks, he was listening to D'angelo and sitting on the couch with his legs wide open. We talked and talked and talked some more, and I could not keep my eyes off his crotch area. He kept smiling each time he caught me looking. He teased me further by adjusting his dick from time to time. I wanted to just kneel down in front of him and unzip his pants and blow the shit out of his dick, but I could see he was tired and so was I. It was almost dawn, so I suggested we go to bed. He took off his pants and shirt and his socks and his boxers. He slept only in the nude, he said. His dick dropped almost to his knee. I said, *Damn!* inside, as my heart pounded and my ass started to get wet and hot and twitchy. I wanted him inside me so bad I could already feel him pushing that big dick in my tight hole over and over again.

Again, I tried to be suggestive with my language but he drifted out in mid-sentence. I smiled and slid next to him. He stirred when he felt me alongside him; his dick popped up and started to move back and forth. He reached out and grabbed me and pulled me close to him. I grabbed his dick and held on to it as it jerked around. I wanted so bad to peek under the sheet and see what was making it so strong and hard and throbbing but I didn't want to violate his sleep. I slept holding his dick in one hand with my head on his shoulder and his arm around me. I don't know why, but it gives me a great deal of comfort to hold on to a man's dick while I sleep, like a teddy bear or favorite blanket. I could hear his heartbeat, and my heartbeat soon synced up with his; it was like we had been sleeping together for years.

The next morning I awoke first. I was greeted by a very hard, throbbing and curious erection peeping out from the sheet. Before I could stop myself, I was down at his crotch. I looked at his beautiful dick. It was thick, with a large vein running down the middle, a pale-pink mushroom head and a slight curve to the right. I kissed it softly along the long shaft and worked my way up to the head. I began to trace the outline of his head with my tongue, which made it jump and spasm. Slowly I took his head past my moist lips and made soft circles around it. Then I scooped his whole head into my mouth and began to suck on it. As I worked my lips farther down his shaft, the warmth of my mouth made Lex stir and then awake. He grabbed the back of my head and began to massage it, while his hips slowly began to grind his dick down my throat. Vocal responses like, "Damn...that's right...it's all yours baby, it's all yours....yeah,

yeah...show that dick what you want," erupted from his mouth as I worked my way farther down the shaft, totally taking his huge, throbbing ten inches in my mouth. I could taste his precum on my tongue and I loved it.

I learned to deep-throat big trade with my first lover, who had ten inches also, so Lex was in for a treat. As my mouth reached his pubic hairs, I used my tongue to play in his hair down there, while he pushed deeper and deeper and harder down my throat. "You can take all my shit, I like that. I love it when my shit is treated right, you feel me?" he said.

"Like this," I said, as I slowly moved down his entire shaft and swallowed his dick and fluttered my tongue in his pubic hair. I held his dick down my throat as long as I could without gagging. It throbbed and beat against my throat.

"Let's get right," Lex said, as he pulled me up to him and kissed me on the lips, his hands massaging my asscheeks real hard. I popped a condom in my mouth and slowly manipulated it onto his head and down his shaft with my lips and tongue. He let out a "Yea, baby...do that shit," which let me know he was pleased with my technique. Then he pulled me onto his hard, muscular body and rolled over, ending up on top of me. His body on my body felt so good I pulled him closer and closer to me. We started to grind together, our dicks rubbing up against each other. My breathing became heavy and my heart raced. "It's time to take care of my business," Lex said, as he pulled back and grabbed my legs and put them on his shoulders and started pushing his dick into my quivering asshole. It was as wet as a pussy but much tighter. I loved the pain I felt as he pushed past my asshole and found his place deep inside me.

He began to grind in a slow circular motion that told me he knew his business. His dick was so big that taking it all on my back was too painful for me, so I asked if I could take it on my stomach. He let my legs down and flipped me over without even pulling his dick out of my ass. Now it felt ten times better, and I let him know. I am a very aggressive bottom, so once we found a mutual rhythm, I began to meet him stroke for stroke. "Damn baby, you throwing that ass back like a pro," he said, as I pushed it back harder and harder.

"Where you at? I am not feeling the love," I teased, trying to turn the heat up.

"Oh, it's like that!" he laughed. Then he grabbed under my pelvis and pulled me closer to him and began to pound in real hard. He continued to pull me closer and pound harder and harder until his body made a slapping noise as it hit my asscheeks. I started to feel him climb deeper inside me and it turned me the fuck out.

I moaned, "Yes, baby...give me that dick...deeper...deeper..." He pulled me onto my knees and pushed my head into the pillow. The room filled with the sound of his body banging against mine. His dick seemed to grow twice as big and I began to pull away, as pain filled my spine.

"Oh, hell no! You wanted it rough, so I'm gonna give it to you just that way," he said. Then he held me in place and wore my ass raw. I screamed and moaned and moaned and screamed into the pillow. Sweat from his chest covered my back and I could hear him grunt like a trapped beast. Suddenly he pulled me up and thrust in one last time, finding his place somewhere between my gut and my heart.

They say when dreams or fantasies come true, it's never as good as you thought. Wrong. Lex was much, much, much better. The best part was when he came. He was very vocal, which I lived for, and it turned me the fuck on until I thought I was going to lose my mind. "Fuck me, Daddy...fuck me harder and deeper. It's all yours..." This seemed to turn Lex out also because the faithful moment arrived quicker than both of us expected. Things started erupting from Lex's mouth. "I'm gonna pop, I'm gonna pop...oh, yeah, I'm popping," Lex yelled as he pounded my ass good. He took one last thrust deep in me and screamed out real loud. I popped him like a bottle of Dom Perignon. As he collapsed on my back, I reached down and grabbed my dick. It was covered with precum and I started jerking it good. It only took seconds before I was screaming out loud myself. Two sweaty, heavy-breathing, animalistic lovers slowly drifted back to sleep.

# THE STICKUP

## Shane Allison

'm going to tell Krishonda that I can't close nights anymore, I said to myself as I pushed a mop lazily across the floor of the dining room. I have no damn social life. This closing at midnight shit isn't going to work for me. I have an 8:00 a.m. class on Mondays and a test in Bio tomorrow. I haven't been able to get any studying done 'cause I've been working this bitch all weekend. I mean, yeah, I told her that my availability is wide open, but I only said that so I could get the job. I have bills to pay and I would have said anything. If she had said, "Eat my pussy" to get the job, I probably would have. I was that desperate.

I figured I would close nights for a couple of months, and then after being on the j-o-b for a while I would flip the script on my availability. I mean, damn, all this closing shit I have to do: sweep, mop, take the trash out, clean these funky-ass bathrooms, put all the food away. We close at ten but sometimes I don't get out of here until midnight. I've only been here five months and already Krishonda's got me closing this bitch by myself, leaving me to do all the work. She comes in every morning before we're open to inspect shit, so I gotta make sure everything is put away and clean. She's the kind of boss that will write you up for the littlest stuff. This guy Rob that works here came in two minutes—two damn minutes!—late and she wrote him up. I caught on quick that if you don't do whatchu need to be doin' she will get rid of your ass with the quickness. Krishonda don't play.

I can see right now I'm not going to be here long. She's either going to fire me or I'ma quit this muthafucka. With all the work she has us doing, I might as well turn in my apron now. I've been here since 12:30 today and my feet are barking. That's what I get for buying cheap-ass shoes.

The sweeping is done, now all I have to do is put the chairs on the tables, clean those nasty-ass bathrooms, mop and put the food away. If I hurry, I might be able to get out of here before midnight.

As I started to stack the chairs, this tall, skinny-ass nigga walked in wearing what looked like a durag over his face. At first I thought he was playing, but when he locked the door behind him and jerked the blinds down over the windows, I thought, *Naw, this fool is serious,* especially when I saw him pull a gun out of one of the pockets of his jacket.

"Move over behind the counter," he told me in a soft, but audible tone. "Dude, are you serious?" I asked.

"Nigga, you want to find out if I'm serious? Move yo' fat ass over behind the counter," he said, moving quickly toward me with the gun aimed at my face. So I did what he wanted. I tried to remember what Krishonda told me if something like this was to go down. "Remain calm; give them what they want, get as much of a description as you possibly can."

But I could barely think straight. My heart dropped down into my nut sac. *Shit, shit, shit-fucking-shit* was all that was going through my head.

"Open the register," he said. I was so freaked out I damn near forgot the code to open up the register. Everything flashed in front of me: my parents, my sister, nieces and nephews, the party the Alpha Taus were throwing next weekend. *I'm gonna die. This crazy muthafucka is going kill me.*

"Hurry the fuck up!" he yelled. I didn't say anything, thinking that he would shoot me just for opening my mouth. I got ahold of myself and managed to get the register open.

"Now move yo' big ass over there," he said, waving me away with the gun. He didn't have to tell me twice. I put my arms up over my head and made my way at the end of the counter. The button for the police was directly under the register, but I was freaking out so I didn't think to press that bitch.

I watched him as he started stuffing fives, tens and twenties in his pockets. I knew there wasn't much. Krishonda didn't want us to keep much money in the register. We take what we need and she told me to never accept bills larger than twenties. I couldn't see his face 'cause it was covered over. He wore baggy jeans with a black tank top. He looked to be the same height as me, maybe a little shorter. I figured he was some bum down on his luck, but he didn't look or smell homeless.

"Damn, this all you got?" he hollered.

"Yeah, that's all they let me keep in the register."

"Shiiiit!" He swore. He looked over at me and stared anxiously like he didn't know whether to bust a cap in my ass or let me go.

He breathed heavy, licking his lips like he had just tasted something sweet.

"Stay there. You move, I'ma shoot you."

He glanced out the window to see if anyone was coming. When he saw that everything was cool, he switched off the last of the lights I had on. I was so scared I thought I was going to piss *and* shit myself. My arms were getting tired. My heart was beating like African drums against my chest. I thought I was going to have a heart attack.

He turned back, pointing his gun at me as he walked back behind the sandwich counter.

"Move to the back," he said. *Oh shit. He's going to kill my ass.* My armpits were dripping with sweat. My legs felt like rubber. I was surprised I could walk. I felt the tip of his gun pointed at my spine.

"Please," was the only word I could say. *Man, you got what you came for. Let me go.*

He held the gun on me, pointed at my chest.

"I won't say nothin'. I swear."

"Shut the fuck up and get on your knees."

"What?"

"You about to find out, fat nigga, that I don't like to repeat myself. Get down on your knees."

I did what I was told.

"Put your arms down."

I let my sore limbs drop down to my side. He moved in closer to me and caressed the side of my face with the barrel of his gun. The black steel felt cold against my skin. My face was pouring with sweat; beads of salty fluid stung my eyes. I felt my glasses slipping off my face, down the bridge of my nose. He pushed them back up with his gun. I prayed that it wouldn't go off.

"Open your mouth," he said, his words muffled through the nylon material.

"Please. Don't do this. I'm sorry." I didn't have anything to apologize for, but I was scared shitless and desperate.

"What I say about repeating myself?"

I pried my lips open and he eased the tip of the gun in past my lips and teeth.

"Don'tchu move, now. I wouldn't want Bad Boy to go off," he said. "That's the name of my gack. *Bad Boy*."

I didn't bat an eyelash.

"Now suck on Bad Boy."

I slowly started to move my mouth up along the shaft of his gun.

"Yeah, that's good. You like that?"

I shut my eyes and nodded my head yes.

"You like hard things in your mouth? I bet you do, faggot."

*Please, Jesus.*

He pushed the gun in deeper.

"Come on, nigga. Suck it."

As he shoved the steel in as far as it would go, I felt myself starting to gag from the obstruction. He eased it out past my lips. Drool dripped like blood from the tip. I exhaled, swallowing my fear like it was nasty-tasting cough medicine.

With the gun pressed against my cheek, he zipped down his roomy jeans with skinny fingers. He smelled faintly of motor oil. I noticed black grit under his fingernails. He reached in and struggled to work his dick out of his drawers, through the opening of his jeans. The smell of ball-sweat bit my senses. His deep-chocolate toned shaft hung like a deli sausage in front of me. The head of his dick was protected with a coat of foreskin.

*What the fuck?*

"You like that?" he whispered. He started playing with it,

easing his foreskin back to expose a bulbous brownish-pink tip. Precum had formed at the teardrop piss-slit. I could see the edges of the cash protruding from the seams of his pockets.

"I want you to suck me."

He traipsed the soft point of his dick along my lips.

"Like that, faggot? Taste that juice."

All I could think about was walking out alive instead of wearing a fuckin' toe tag.

"Open up," he said.

"Wider." He stuffed his thickness into my mouth. I wrapped my lips around the shaft and started to suck.

"Yeah, good, like that."

I started to move my wet lips up along his appendage. The taste of sweat was immediate, the stench of motor oil wavering. I started to gag.

"You puke on me, faggot and I'll put one in your shoulder." I pushed his sweat and dick-cheese down my throat.

"C'mon," he said, tapping his gun on my shoulder. "I know your pretty-ass can suck a dick better than that."

I hugged his donkey-hung dick tighter in my mouth.

"Fuck yeah. That's wha'ssup." He stumbled closer, feeding me inch after fat inch.

"Suck my damn dick, faggot."

I kept my eyes closed to keep the sweat from burning them. He slipped his dick out and said, "Suck my balls."

I started to lick his funky-ass balls. They smelled and tasted like they hadn't seen soap and water in days, maybe weeks. I throated sweat and spit. His nuts hung low to my chin. I took them into my mouth.

"I like having my balls sucked," he said as he thumped his dick against my face.

"Eat my nuts, punk."

My glasses slipped off my face. I picked them up off the floor to save them from getting broken. Everything was blurry.

"What? You just going to leave this dick hangin', fat boy?" He forced it back into my mouth. His pubes brushed against my face. The muscles in my jaw started to tighten and ache. I had never taken a dick that was as big as his.

"Damn, you suck dick better than my shorty." I was able to relax my body, slow my heartbeat. The balls of my knees were hurting. Muscles in me were on fire.

His thrusts started to quicken. I struggled to keep up.

"Ready for this nut?" he asked, like I had a choice. With the gun in his hand, he pressed my head down on his dick, sliding in and back out. I kept my lips tight, hugging his meat.

*Hope he don't pull that trigger when he comes.*

"Suck it. Suck that dick, nigga," he demanded as he fucked my throat.

"Oh shit. Here I come."

My mouth and throat filled with cum.

"Take that nut, nigga."

It took a couple of gulps to get his seed down.

He pushed me back against the stainless-steel door of the freezer. I collapsed on the floor of the kitchen I had not gotten around to mopping. His dick was soaked, leaking dapples of spit and cum.

I could make him out through blurred sight, working his dick back into his jeans. As I tried to gather myself, he pressed the gun in my chest.

"Don't move." He felt at my pockets and fished out my wallet. He flipped it open.

"Derrick Stalworth. Now I know where to find you if I see anything about me in the papers." The muscles in my body were screaming.

"Wait five minutes and then you can get up."

I was too scared to move. I heard the door being unlocked and then closing. I wiped the sweat from my face and put on my glasses. I started to calm down; things started to slow. I sat up against the freezer with a slip of a smile that had formed across my face.

*Damn, what just happened?*

# NO RULES
# (BUTT ONE)

## Bob Masters

Justin Maxwell was driving his beater in the backcountry of Indiana. Twenty years old and feeling about forty, Justin was driving to forget about life for a while. His parents were on his back about making something of himself. He did realize that he needed to do something with his life. The hard part was figuring out what that was supposed to be. He had tried to make it in junior college, but that just wasn't for him. He had been helping his pa around the farm, but he knew he couldn't stay there forever. It seemed like the whole world was trying to tell him to be an adult. But he just didn't feel like being what folks around Spencer understood adult to be. He didn't want to get married and have kids and be stuck in some Podunk town like Spencer, Indiana for the rest of his life.

Memories of the irresponsible days of his youth had been crowding in upon him relentlessly, and so he had jumped into his '69 Impala and taken off down Highway 231. He loved the feel of the wheel as he drove down the familiar road. He had saved up every dime he had made since high school to buy the vintage car. It was the one thing in the world that he could call his own. The beginnings of carefree feelings were just starting when thoughts of what lay ahead of him in life intruded once more. He just couldn't shake a sense of life turning ugly for him, only he couldn't name precisely why. The car, as if confirming his sense of impending doom, began to shudder and tremble. Seconds later, a loud bang shook the car and the engine died. He struggled with the failed power-steering to guide it to the side of the road and put it in park.

He got out, cursing under his breath, and opened the hood to check the engine. Nothing looked wrong. He always kept the oil and water filled. Getting back in the car, he turned the key a few times, but to no avail. Staring into the summer sky, Justin felt his world was truly crashing around him. Welcome to nowhere, Indiana. His private paradise now seemed more like a small piece of hell. There wouldn't be a house or gas station within miles. He got out and thought about which direction to start hiking. He had been on the road about twenty minutes. Freedom was somewhere south; Spencer, his home, was to the north. He had no idea which was closer, but decided to head north. Maybe his folks would miss him, or a neighbor would drive by.

Bucky Russo was a biker boy, bad to the bone, but only because he liked to buck society's conventions. That's how he came by his nickname, in fact. He was always giving the finger to authority or expectations of any kind. He liked to transgress boundaries and that included sexual ones. He never identified with any group, gay or straight, and he had never had a long-term relationship. He had never joined a motorcycle gang, though he looked like a natural. Bucky was a loner, not because he couldn't fit in, but because he didn't want to. What he did want to do was hit the open road on his souped-up chopper decked out with a deep-purple finish and sky-high handlebars. The bright silver engine sat forward of his low-slung seat and gave him plenty of horsepower to tool down any damn road he wanted to. He accentuated his big, muscular frame with tight-fitting jeans covered by leather chaps. He only wore a leather mesh vest on his upper torso, and he eschewed the protection of a helmet. He knew of the dangers involved; he just didn't care. He valued quality, not quantity of life. Parents, school, even a few run-ins with the police had never convinced him otherwise.

Justin was beginning to get hungry and tired as he tromped through the torrid summer heat. He did feel glad that he had chosen to wear his denim cut-offs, for the loose fit allowed a little breeze to waft up the opening between his thighs and the fabric. But his underwear soon became sopping wet with sweat. He slipped them and his pants down his legs and doffed the dripping skivvies into the brush on the side of the road. Pulling up his pants, he realized that he might not see anyone by night-fall. He wasn't worried about getting cold, but he would have to sleep on the ground and get eaten alive by insects. And now that his underpants were gone, his crotch would be exposed to bugs. His sandals kept his feet cool, but the thongs started to dig into the flesh between his toes as he hiked down the blistering highway.

Justin was just about to despair of ever seeing help when he heard a distant rumble. It was loud and deep, reverberating through the stillness of the summer air like a jackhammer. Birds darted out of nearby trees as the cacophony grew nearer, and Justin moved instinctively to the side of the road. He saw a cloud of dust in the distance but that was soon erased as a vague chimera of purple began to coalesce into the shape of monster-chopper of obscene proportions. The front wheels protruded some two to three feet in front of the chassis, and the handlebars looked similarly out of proportion. Justin was astonished and only unconsciously, albeit belatedly, stuck out his thumb when the bike was almost past him. The sparkling silver and purple low-rider skidded to a stop. A large, muscular man who looked about twice his size sat there with a bemused expression on his face. Justin noticed how his bronze biceps glistened with sweat in the glaring summer sun. He wondered if he had done the right thing in brazenly sticking out his thumb. He should have known better than to hitchhike. He knew it wasn't safe. But the feeling in the pit of his stomach and the fear of spending the night out in the open had propelled his thumb up and out. Now a big dude with a huge purple chopper was looking him up and down like he was some fool out for a walk without proper protection.

"Hey, son! What in hell-blazes are you doing out here in the middle of nowhere?"

"Car broke down. I need a ride."

"Ever been on a chopper before?"

"No, sir"

"Name's Bucky, boy. I don't like that 'sir' shit. Makes me feel old. Well, I guess I can't leave you to bake out here in the Indiana sunshine. Come on over."

Justin ambled over to the humming chopper as Bucky reached behind the other side to open a bag and retrieve a little pad with suction cups on the bottom.

"You can't wear those," said Bucky, pointing at Justin's feet. "And you got to put your feet up on these," he said as he flipped down two pedal-like protrusions on each side of the cycle. "And this here is your seat," he said as he plopped the suction cups halfway down the rear fender. "Climb on."

Justin kicked off his sandals and plopped his butt down on the surprisingly comfortable gel-filled pad. Only it was positioned so that his body was jutted forward into Bucky's muscular backside.

"Now, you sit there and don't move, don't lean, and keep quiet," the big man instructed him. "And I need you to put your arms around my waist."

Bucky unzipped his vest and grabbed Justin's hands and brought them forward so they were joined just over the man's slightly hairy belly.

"Ready?" shouted Bucky as he revved the engine. "Hold on tight!"

With that the machine erupted in a roar that filled the air like a thunderbolt. Gravel spun out from underneath them and Justin felt his hands sink into the man's stomach as his body was wrenched back. It was a total blur of noise and panic mixed with excitement as they covered the distance to Justin's car in less than two minutes. Bucky slowed down beside the Impala.

"That your car?"

"Yep, was, that is."

"What happened?"

"Dunno, heard a loud clang and the engine died."

"Sounds like you blew a rod. Too bad, you could have fixed that baby up with a new engine and jacked it up a few feet. Too late now. So, where are you from? Need a ride home?"

Flashes of pictures of his boring and stressful home life passed through Justin's mind. He didn't want to have to explain about the car. This Bucky fellow had not judged him for what happened. But his parents would.

"Spencer is where I come from. How 'bout you?"

"Me? Bloomington is where I sleep. Spend most of my time on the road. Do some cycle repairs for money."

"I'm glad you drove by. Never been on a motorcycle before."

"Never, man?'

"No, Spencer is kind of boring. We don't see many purple choppers!"

"How do you like it?"                                            \

"I love it. I would love to ride with you all day. I 'spose you have better things to do than cart my ass around, though."

"Well, don't put words in my mouth. Bucky don't follow no rules. Maybe I want you to ride with me all day."

Justin paused and reviewed his life up to this point, short order style. He was twenty, dammit. It was time he lived. He could explain about the car to his parents later.

"Well, I am all for it if you are!" he challenged.

"Then hold on, son, we're going for a ride!"

The engine roared and they spun out away from his broken-down old car and his broken-down old life. They rode in the summer sun together, down Highway 231 until they reached the 54 East interchange. All the while, Justin enjoyed the view with someone else doing the driving for a change. The open environment of the motorcycle was unlike anything he had ever experienced, and he wasn't sure if it was the excitement of this or the vibrations that continually shook his legs that made his cock start to stiffen. His cock was pressed against Bucky's ass and Justin hoped he wouldn't have to explain away his hard-on. But Bucky said nothing.

They eventually pulled onto Highway 54, which was more of a major highway, and Bucky really opened the throttle and showed what his purple monster could do. They zipped past cars and trucks and the sensation was unbelievable. It was a freedom that Justin had never experienced. By the time they reached Highway 37 North, the sun had started to set. This was the road to Bloomington, and after a while a sky full of stars erupted into view. That was one of the best features of living in this rural part of Indiana. Justin was enjoying the ride, the beautiful stars and a sense of boundaries dropping away from him when he felt his hand suddenly being gently removed from Bucky's stomach and lowered down between his legs. Justin felt his fingers come in contact with a warm shaft of flesh that could only be the muscleman's cock. Shocked at first, Justin allowed the sensation of the forbidden to settle into his mind. He felt his breath give, and the closeness of his body propped up against the huge man's back, with the man's muscular ass shoved tightly against his own crotch, made his own cock grow hard in response. Seduced on a motorcycle! Justin laughed to himself and wondered how he could let the man know that he liked what was happening. He saw the back of Bucky's neck as the wind blew his longish blond hair away from his head. Justin leaned forward and lightly kissed the flesh there. Bucky removed his hand from Justin's and reached back to pat his thigh.

They said nothing for the next few miles until Bucky pulled onto a little dirt road that jutted off the highway toward the huge forest preserve that held Monroe Lake State Park. It was a State Park, but the huge expanse held many small roads and areas like this one that were rarely used except by hunters and fishermen. The road soon meandered into little more than a dirt trail and Bucky slowed the chopper to a crawl and used parking lights only as they entered an area of widely spaced pine trees.

"I know the perfect place to watch the stars. And we can spend the night here, if you want," said the muscular motorcyclist.

"It's beautiful. I used to vacation here when I was little."

Bucky only chuckled and let the chopper coast a few hundred feet through the pines until the sound of water could be heard. He parked it and climbed off, offering Justin his hand in climbing down from his perch. Justin let Bucky take him by the hand as they walked together toward the water. Soon they were standing before an extension of the lake system that was far away from any kind of tourist site. The moonlight reflected in the water like a mirror. Bucky put his arms around Justin and drew him close to his muscle-bound body.

"I don't want you to feel you have to do anything you don't want to, Justin. But I want to spend the night with you. See, I don't follow any rules. Only what my heart tells me. And my heart tells me you need some grown-up lovin'."

Justin felt a thrill course up and down his spine and his body began to tremble a little. "I...I...ain't done this kind of thing before, Bucky, but I...think I want to, with you."

Bucky embraced and kissed the young man, thrusting his tongue between his lips. He probed gently at first, slowly increasing the potency of his oral exploration with deeper and more sensuous manipulations of his tongue inside the handsome youngster's mouth. Justin soon began to moan and return his kisses, but Bucky broke free and rained kisses all over his face and eyes instead. He then swept Justin off his feet and carried him in his powerful arms to the lake embankment. He laid him down on the soft, pine-needle flooring and proceeded to strip off his own clothes, from his leather boots and chaps to his jeans and vest, which he spread out on the ground and motioned Justin to lie atop. Justin moved himself onto the makeshift bedding and Bucky reached down and undid his denim shorts. Justin lifted his midsection to allow Bucky greater ease in taking them off. When he lowered his body, his erect cock plopped against his down-covered waist. Bucky's own cock was rock hard and sprouting out the top of his white briefs gleaming in the moonlight. They regarded each other's naked beauty for a moment. Then Bucky abruptly lay down on top of Justin and began to gently grind his nakedness against the handsome boy's.

To Justin, it felt like a Greek god had kidnapped him and was now pressing his otherworldly frame against him. Every inch of flesh touching his own sent waves of sexual delight pulsing throughout his being. It felt as if all the pain and loneliness of the past few years was being rubbed away. He could feel his own hunger for Bucky's touch rising from within his bones and sinews. He surrendered himself to this stranger. A stranger who was claiming him, in fact, from an alienation whose nature he had not fully realized.

"Oh, Bucky, I love you," spilled out his mouth.

Bucky drew himself up and looked into Justin's eyes. "Is this your first time, Justin?"

"I haven't even kissed a girl, Bucky."

"Well, then, I promise to go easy on you. I kind of like what I heard, though"—and before Justin could respond, Bucky reached down and pulled his underwear off. He then pressed his raging cock against Justin's crotch and let their cocks touch with an electric tension that notched up the lust factor. Bucky then reared up on his haunches and scooped up Justin's well-formed legs. He proceeded to kiss his inner thighs, his calves, and finally, taking each foot in turn, suck Justin's toes while he expertly caressed his legs. Bucky paused in his lovemaking and said, "I want to show you what my cock can do for you, Justin. But since this is your first time, I am going to start off slow. Why don't you lie on your back and let me show you?"

Justin languidly rolled over and positioned his lithesome body so that his ass protruded gingerly into the clean, crisp forest air. Bucky situated himself between those enticing thighs and plunged his face into the heretofore unplucked fruit that lay on offer. He gently, lovingly began to tongue the pink flesh of Justin's ass. Working his magic to both relax and excite, Bucky was soon satisfied as Justin ground his cock against the leather bedding and his ass wiggled uncontrollably. Bucky's tonguing had invaded his inner universe. Slowly, the bud of this special flower was opening. Bucky spread his asscheeks gently apart as he thrust his tongue inside the quivering hole. He then slicked his index finger with saliva and worked it inside. When he felt Justin's sphincter relax, he spit into his palm and slathered up his turgid cock until it glistened wetly in the pale night air. He placed the tip against the target and pushed until the tip of his fuck-tool popped inside. Justin shuddered and groaned but finally relaxed. They repeated this sequence until Bucky's cock was all the way inside. Justin groaned and involuntarily squeezed the hard cock inside him, causing Bucky to increase his tempo more and more until he was lustily fucking the virgin. Bucky wanted to make it special, so he held back from letting his sperm shoot. He lowered his body atop Justin and kissed him while he drove his cock to the hilt and gyrated it with cork-screw motions. He felt his lover's body tremble and buck as hot ribbons of cum erupted between their sweaty bodies. That sent Bucky into completely involuntary orgasm, his sperm erupting in spurt after spurt of white-hot man-juice in Justin's belly, his ass muscles contracting and pulsing with animal need.

Justin knew he would never return home. Bucky knew he would no longer be a loner. It would be trouble for both of them. But that was what love was like. Trouble. A trouble that might last a lifetime. They were both brave enough to face it.

# BOONEY'S HUNTER

## Salome Wilde

The tale of why Boy Two-Blood gave up his title as Booney's Hunter isn't often told, but when it is, people stop and listen. The story says something about life and freedom and maybe even a little about settling down, but not the usual variety. Boy certainly wasn't the romantic kind, for one, and his relationship with Adam Spillman couldn't by any stretch be called a marriage. Still, Boy stopped being the town's avenging angel—or devil—around 1802, and never again was he seen carrying a beaten, hog-tied young Booney man over his shoulder into his broken-down cabin in the woods on a moonless night.

Most townsfolk know Boy's story well enough, though some say it's more folktale than fact. Boy was said to be the bastard orphan son of an escaped slave and a mixed-blood Cherokee woman named Mary Two-Blood, two strangers who fucked like beautiful animals to feel alive on the banks of the Tennessee River just south of the Virginia border one hot July day before parting forever as one fled north and the other west. The slave was a product of a godless coupling forced by a master on his female property. His father, owner of many a creature who did his bidding or died at the overseer's whip or gun, called this particular babe "Lucky," christening his dubiously honored status as the one-hundredth slave on the plantation. The moniker also reflected the master's gratitude that the babe was born especially dark-skinned, preventing his wife—a frail and jealous woman—from knowing of his proclivities in the grubby slave cabins down by the fields. But "Lucky" had another meaning for the boy who grew to a man with this soubriquet. He fled the plantation, never to return; and though he bore guilt for not being able to take his strong-eyed mother with him nor ever marrying or knowing the pleasures of parenthood, he did in fact father a child, an infamous child the likes of which never was or would be seen again in this wicked world. He fathered Boy.

Mary Two-Blood was Boy's mother. She had herself been born of a strange love, one between a Cherokee man and a plantation owner's wife who found sanctuary within a small branch of the tribe. The woman's husband—who was not the father of Lucky but certainly could have been—forever spoke of his beloved Charity having been "kidnapped by savages" and demanded her safe return by local authorities. When the sheriff proved inept, he even spent fairly respectable amounts of cash in hiring thugs to bring her home. But Charity was never found, having given her fate over to the handsome Degotoga, whose name meant "Standing Together" in Cherokee, and who lived up to that promise. Together, they found love and bore a child, pale and of her mother's nervous disposition. Though Degotoga wanted to call her Ayita, "First to Dance," Charity saw the way the tribe frowned at her milky white skin and blue eyes, and so, to protect her according to Charity's Christian upbringing, she was called Mary, though the others called her Two-Blood.

Because such a history is as gnarled as an old live-oak and it is the child of Lucky and Mary who concerns us in this hunter's tale, it should suffice to say that after the tryst by the river, Mary never saw Lucky again. That lithe youth fled north of the Mason-Dixon and labored—this time for pay—in the fields of Pennsylvania until he died, feeling as lucky as hard labor and a lonely life could make him. The lover he took that one sweltering summer day, however, did not flee. She wandered only a few hours west until she found an abandoned cabin in the mountains above what would soon become the town of Booney, named for that intrepid adventurer Daniel Boone. No one came looking for her. One could lay blame, but to what end? Mary found living alone was no less lonely than watching her mother bear child after child, growing ever more radiant and strong with Degotoga's love. The two had eyes for none but each other, and Mary washed dirty baby clothes and shrank into herself until the day she grew bold enough to flee.

In her tiny cabin, with just enough wood and dried meat to survive the winter, Mary Two-Blood swelled with life as the leaves turned. Pregnancy surprised her no more than the encounter in the woods itself, for Mary had learned to take life as it came. She ran her fingers over the pages of the Bible she'd stolen from her mother's bedside when she fled the home she'd grown up in. Since she had never learned to read, it was more a self-comforting ritual than any practice of faith or edification, but it soothed her. When her child was born, she had a desire to name it for its father, who had been kind to her after he gave her his seed. He had held her close and whispered wisdom in her small ear: "Live free or die trying." But she didn't know his name, his words made little sense in the context of her small existence, and what she remembered most was the sheen of sweat on his brow and the beautiful low noises he made as he planted his hardness inside her and claimed an innocence she had no use for. When at last she gave birth, it was in solitude, and the babe was neither baptized nor even truly named. "Boy," Mary called her son, and Boy he always remained. That is, until he also became known as Booney's Hunter.

Death took Mary Two-Blood through some unnamed illness when her son was only twelve, but already he had become self-sufficient, learning to hunt with slingshot and trap, to skin game and to bring pelts to town to fetch, with sullen, downturned eyes, the provisions and coin they brought. He'd stop on the way back to the lonely cabin to fetch the moonshine his mother demanded, and learned a taste for hard liquor before she passed. Fortunately, the blood of hard drinkers was thin in his veins. Instead, Boy grew strong and limber, with a temperament more even than his mother, but as devoted to living free as the father he never knew.

By the time he was twenty, Boy was hunting with knife, bow, and homemade traps of fine craftsmanship. He taught himself to tan hides, and he could often be seen running among the trees in fine buckskin and fur hat, pursuing deer and wolf, coyote and even bear. The pelts brought in money to buy better weapons, including a gun and shot he rarely used, eggs and milk and greens, and the town's morbid attention. He was an unwashed beast and not one for conversation, always averting his gaze and replying with little more than "Yep" or "Nope," regardless of topic. It wasn't that he was humble, though he was far from arrogant. Instead, the burly young man was simply uninterested in the world beyond his cabin and hunting.

The spring of his twenty-second year, however, a change came to Boy Two-Blood's life. James Robert Leary, the wealth-

iest horse dealer in the county, came to call. He had locals
guide him up the mountain, then had them wait a ways back
with their horses. He dismounted and approached the rickety
little cabin, then rapped hard on the old wooden door. It swung
open. The catch no longer held, it seemed, and Boy saw no
reason to fix it. The creak woke him from his afternoon rest,
however—for Boy rose before sunrise to fish and hunt, and
enjoyed a nap in the cool of his home when the sun was hottest.
"Who's there?" called Boy, grabbing his knife and coming off
his bed in a crouch.

"Pardon me," replied Leary, raising his hands to show he
meant no harm and smiling warmly. "I'm here to make you an
offer, son." He bowed. If Leary smelled the sickly-sweet odor of
brains slathered on hides stretched from one end of the cabin to
the other and the ammonia tang of urine for soaking them, his
expression did not betray it. He might have been greeting the
newly elected president Mr. Thomas Jefferson himself, he was
so polite and respectful.

Boy didn't know what to make of it. So little prolonged
contact with his fellow humans had left him more confused
than wary in this situation. He rose and stepped into the light,
though he didn't drop his knife. "What offer?" he asked.

Leary shifted in his boots. He was unaccustomed to doing
business in a doorway with an unwashed, unshaven man in
nothing but his undershorts, brandishing a knife no less—
though he had no desire to be asked inside. Despite the rough-
ness, the man was impressive: tall and solidly muscled, dark
in eyes and skin. If Leary wasn't entirely convinced Boy Two-
Blood had never harmed a man in his life, he'd have fled the
minute that knife glinted. Instead, he cleared his throat. "Well,
son," he began, "I have myself a little problem, and I think you
can help me."

"What problem?" Boy prodded, neither moving nor changing his expression.

Leary faced directness with directness, even if it wasn't his preferred method of discourse. "Well, it's about one of my hands, Rafe Owens," he continued, eyes narrowing. Just saying the name clearly angered him. "The skunk tried to run off with my daughter, Maylene."

Boy showed no reaction to the crime, though he did note the way Leary was now grinding his teeth. "What's that gotta do with me?" he asked, perhaps the longest question he'd ever posed aloud.

"You're good with hunting and trapping," Leary replied. "You know how to catch a beast and make it pay."

"Pay?" Boy echoed. "I jus' hunt. Critters don' do me no harm."

Leary nodded vigorously. "And that's what I want you to do for me. Rafe Owens was last seen on your mountain. I want you to hunt him."

Boy cocked his head and scratched his stubbly cheek. His brain labored to make sense of what Leary was asking. "Hunt... Rafe Owens?" Why would a man hunt a man?

"I don't want him killed," Leary qualified, once again putting up a hand, as if to ward off misunderstanding. No, Leary had been involved in a hanging or two in his time, but this was Andrew Owens's child, and he had no intention of being held responsible for the boy's death. At very least, if news got out he'd hired someone to kill Rafe, it'd be bad for business. And business was everything to Leary—much to the dismay of his wife, six children and two mistresses. "I just want you to scare him. Scare him good."

Boy weighed the issue in his mind as best he could. As he saw it, one man wanted another man hurt but not killed, shamed maybe, for doing the first man wrong. Something about a woman. Thoughts of his mother—the only woman he ever really knew—flitted through his mind. How would he feel if someone tried to take her away from him? Well, God had. But he wasn't angry at God. He didn't really know who God rightly was. But when he was a boy, a man selling things from a wagon had come to their cabin, and he'd had an instinctive fear the man might put his Mama in the wagon and take her away. It was terrible, and he'd run out with his slingshot and threatened to kill the man if he didn't get off their land right then and there. It had made his mother laugh, and the sound, though unfamiliar, warmed him. Yes, Boy knew how to scare someone. "What's in it for me?"

Leary smiled. This was going better than he'd expected. He'd been prepped by Agnes at the general store, who told him what Boy bought when he came down monthly from the mountain with his pelts and leather. Leary held out a basket of eggs, some apples and two loaves of fresh brown bread. "You teach Rafe Owens a good lesson he'll never forget, and you'll have all this—and all the eggs you can eat for a year."

Boy laughed, or opened his wide mouth and made a hoot more of animal than man. The offer suited him well, right well indeed. "You got y'self a deal, mister," he said, switching the blade from right hand to left and extending his hand for a shake, the gesture he'd learned when bargaining to sell the products of his hunting.

And that was how Boy Two-Blood began his career as the Hunter. Rafe Owens was caught, beaten, hog-tied and dragged back to the cabin to have other things done to his person that he never spoke of to his dying day. After him came Lou Drummond. Then Nate Hollings. Then Drew Oldham. One by one, each young white man faced the Hunter's punishment for his crime—most involving misdeeds with the unmarried daughters of the town—and left the cabin bruised and bent in mind and body. None were killed, some fled the county after and a few had to be taught their lesson more than once, but not one ever told the details of what had happened up there on the mountain, in Boy Two-Blood's wretched cabin in the woods.

Strangely enough, Boy's profitable career ceased forever, in a most unexpected way. By the end of his time as a hunter of men, he'd gained no money—for he wanted none—but attained an incredible supply of comestibles, ample wood for his fire, excellent tools, costly and beautiful weapons, a canary in a cage and a magnificent, well-saddled horse. He'd also learned the art of handling men's bodies better than he'd ever expected and with more pleasure than wrestling any bear or roping any deer. He could hunt, catch and bind a man so fast he barely knew what hit him. However, in the end, Boy met his match.

Perhaps it shouldn't be surprising that, from the moment he was given the job of catching and punishing the stranger Adam Spillman for his crimes, Booney's Hunter felt a shudder run through him. The name was unfamiliar, but then, so were almost all of them. It was just another young man accused of illicit deeds against the so-called fair sex. This time, though, they couldn't give him the name of the woman who'd been wronged. And the formal request for his services came from Leary, whom he'd not dealt with since that first meeting several years earlier. Leary's eyes were shifty now, and Boy felt something wasn't right. "What'd you say he done again?" Boy asked, hoping to have this cleared up so he could enjoy the hunt.

"Oh, he's a terrible one," Leary enthused. "No woman in this town is safe."

This seemed on a scale bigger than the Hunter had ever faced. "*No* woman?"

Leary shook his head. There was menace in his gaze that Boy instinctively responded to, though what it meant he was still unsure. "No woman." When Boy stroked his chin, looking more thoughtful than he actually was, it seemed to frighten Leary, who confided in a low, conspiratorial tone, "He's a Jew."

Boy nodded slowly. He had not an idea in the world what a Jew was, but clearly, it was something terrible. "I best take care of him, then," he said gravely.

The deal was struck, and Boy was given information about the last known whereabouts of the renegade Jew. Apparently, the man had been shacked up with Belle Parsons after they'd thrown him out of Mrs. Murphy's boarding house. The poor widow had no idea the man was a dirty Jew or she'd have thrown him out herself, she made clear. But old Miss Lucy Belle Parsons took him into her place, and she had to know. Jonathan Oldman said he'd told her himself to watch out for a Jew looking for lodgings when he saw her at church the previous Sunday. And she'd thanked him for his warning and everything.

Boy wasn't used to coming into town to do his work. Most often, the men were chased up into the woods where he'd literally hunt them down. Occasionally, they'd be left, already beaten some, outside his door. That was less sport, but he still gave his special brand of punishment. This one, though, this Adam Spillman the Jew, was more trouble than usual. With much complaint—largely in the form of grunts and groans as he washed himself a little and put on his finest leathers and rode to town on his horse—he came to Miss Parsons's boarding house and knocked on the door.

Startled by the size and shape and darkness of the mountain man, Miss Parsons uttered a "Mercy me!" before stepping back from the doorway and inviting Boy in for supper. She'd just put down the evening meal and never turned a stranger away, though she thought in the back of her aging mind that perhaps she did know this man, had seen him once or twice around town. But her eyes weren't as good as they once were, and it seemed safest to just welcome him in. "Why don't you come join me and my new lodger, Mr. Spillman, for a bite?"

The invitation—the first he'd received in his life—left Boy speechless. But the mention of the name Spillman made him mutter, "Thank you, ma'am," take off his hat, scrape off the bottoms of his boots and enter. He'd get a chance to see this Jew up close, to measure his prey before the hunt began. And, besides, the smell of fried chicken and cornbread was too sweet to turn down.

A slender man with large, startlingly green eyes looked up at him from the table, then rose. His dress was simple but elegant, his features pleasant but unremarkable. When his gaze met Boy's however, something strange happened. The man stuttered his greeting, and Boy's mouth opened and stayed that way for a moment before he shut it again and swallowed, hard. The man looked so gentle that with longer hair and a dress he might be mistaken for a girl. But then, the firmness of his jaw and the way he looked straight on at Boy was all man. Plain and simply, Boy had never encountered anything like Adam Spillman in his life. *So this is what a Jew is*, he thought to himself as he sat down and tucked a napkin under his chin.

Boy's ignorance of the Jewish faith meant that his observation lacked the stereotype and superstition of those who had sought his services to scare Spillman out of town. There was no notice of the lack of a hooked nose, for example, nor was there concern that he had no beard nor kept his head covered at the table. As he ate, his touch was nimble but not greedy. The meal, in fact, passed quietly and pleasantly with neither old Miss Parsons in her black lace nor Boy Two-Blood in his leathers passing the slightest judgment on the very pleasant and quite undirty Jew at the table.

Mostly, for Boy, there was confusion. Or at least that is how he interpreted his emotions in his dull way. His observation of how neatly this Spillman ate his chicken was keen, as was his study of the seeming genuineness of his smile when Miss Parsons offered him another helping of mustard greens. And it was then that conversation began. "That's a new recipe I used for the greens," Miss Parsons told Boy, as if he'd often supped with her before. "Mr. Spillman isn't partial to ham," she explained.

"That so?" Boy responded, cocking his head like a dog, wondering if perhaps there was something important in that. After all, didn't every man like pig? He shoveled another thickly buttered bit of cornbread into his mouth and chewed thoughtfully. Then he tasted the greens again. He boiled his own with bacon grease, when he took the time to cook anything more than meat, but these were nicer. "Right tasty," he said in praise to Miss Parsons with a little nod, not wanting to appear single-mindedly focused on the Jew. But the next moment he pointed his fork in the man's direction. "You like deer, Spillman?" he inquired, thinking about the carcass he had hanging in the closet at home that he used for meat storage rather than clothes, which mostly just lay in a pile beside his bed.

The response was another smile that made the food swell like a lump in Boy's stomach. He felt his heart beat a little faster and wondered if Jews could use magic like some Negroes knew voodoo. "I regret not," Spillman said in a bright, clear voice with the touch of an accent Boy couldn't place. "Though I do love chicken," he added, turning and toasting Miss Parsons with his water glass, "especially the way you cook it, ma'am."

Boy couldn't deny the chicken was delicious. The batter was rich and crunchy and the flesh so tender it practically slid off the bones. The kind he usually ate was what was brought to his cabin as pay for his hunting efforts or what he bought now and then in trade for pelts or hides. It occurred to Boy that he'd been getting the toughest birds and the last of the batch most of the time. And it brought a fire to his eyes.

"Something wrong?" Spillman asked as they sipped coffee in the parlor after the meal, while Miss Parsons took up the dishes.

Boy had been silent, but he hadn't known his sullenness was obvious to anyone but him. He was mentally tallying the way his dozen eggs always had several old and puny ones. The last coil of rope he was given had the smell of horse on it, too, like it had been already used. Though he wasn't sure enough as to be definite about it, Boy Two-Blood was coming to the profound conclusion that he wasn't being done right by lately. He blinked up at the Jew, whose look of concern seemed to him as warm as a mother's. Rather than comfort him, however, the expression infuriated him. He felt a hint of ridicule in the smile now, more than a touch of condescension. Well, Boy Two-Blood may not have been refined or well-spoken, and he may have been taken for a fool by the townsfolk a time or two, but he was Booney's Hunter and he could show this Jew—whatever in hell that was—what it meant to be Booney's Hunter.

He clanked his cup down on the side table, sloshing a bit of the warm, brown liquid—that tasted far better than anything he ever made—onto an ornately crocheted doily, and peered quickly toward the dining room, noting that Miss Parsons had cleared everything away and was still making dish-cleaning noises in the kitchen. He strode to the blue armchair with its lace antimacassars where Spillman sat, green eyes wide in apprehension, and took out the soiled rag that served as his handkerchief to shove it into the Jew's mouth before throwing him over his shoulder like a side of beef. Spillman's coffee cup crashed to the floor and the two were out the door before Miss Parsons could even poke out her head to ask if everything was all right.

The triumph Boy usually felt at slinging his prey over his horse's rump and tying wrists and ankles was dulled by Spillman's lack of resistance. The man wasn't fighting back...at all. Of course, he couldn't speak, not with a wad of cloth in his mouth, but that shouldn't have stopped him from some serious grunting, not to mention kicking and flailing. All the others had. Spillman wasn't totally limp, Boy qualified in his mind, as they galloped off to his cabin against a bright, starry sky. If he didn't know better, he might have said the man was almost helping him. He frowned and kicked his horse—a swift and sleek mount he prized but hadn't bothered to name—to get them home faster. He had the feeling of being tricked, but he couldn't say exactly how or by whom. Was this some plan of Leary's? Perhaps the Sheriff had put him up to this. Or maybe it was Spillman himself. Maybe sly trickery was a Jew's way, though he doubted it. While something was definitely wrong here, Spillman didn't have the feel of a swindler about him. In fact, the way his eyes followed Boy as he was bound and steadied and the way his dark-lashed eyelids drifted shut stirred the mountain man in ways he couldn't name.

Boy also couldn't say what made him forego the beating of the Jew. That's what Leary wanted, after all: a vicious beating after which he'd be left on the road outside of town. If Leary or any of the other townsmen knew Boy was using his cock as well as his fists as a weapon, they certainly never said so. All they wanted were results, and Boy brought results. As Spillman was dropped to slump in the old chair in the corner of the cabin, wrists and ankles still bound, he seemed to be waiting for something. Boy paced before him in the dim light of a single candle, whip in hand and prick plenty hard. Why was he hesitating?

Spillman lifted his head and implored with his eyes, and Boy found himself drifting over to take out the rag. The Jew coughed a few times then hoarsely expressed gratitude. Boy bit his lip and scuffed a heel like a schoolboy before fetching a cracked cup of tepid water. He held it up to Spillman's lips and the man drank. "I gotta teach you a lesson," Boy said, softly, almost apologetically, putting the cup down on the floor between them.

"I understand," said Spillman calmly. Boy found not a hint of mirth in his eyes, nor did he seem to expect rescue. But he wasn't so dull as to seem resigned to his fate either.

Boy scratched his head. "You understand? Well, I don't." And then he asked a question he'd never asked of his prey before. "Did you really do what they say you done?"

Spillman furrowed his brow. "Depends, I guess. What am I supposed to have done?"

Boy flushed a little. As rough and crass as he seemed to most and perhaps actually was, he found the subject of women awkward at best. "You know," he insisted. "Doin' wrong by some of the townsfolk." When Spillman continued to stare, he added hastily, "Carryin' on with…women."

Spillman's expression turned from incomprehension to shock to outright mirth. He opened his mouth and laughed. Laughed good and hard and long, despite his bonds and despite the impending beating he faced in a filthy little hovel in the woods.

Boy flushed harder. Had he said something funny? Was the Jew a lunatic as well as a seducer? He took the man's chin in his iron grip and leaned in to glare hard into those smiling eyes. "It ain't a matter for jest," he growled, trying to get some control over the situation.

Spillman sobered instantly. "No," he agreed quickly, showing he felt the menace he faced for real. "I didn't mean…" His voice trailed off as he slowly blinked his shining eyes and bit his lip.

Boy wanted to understand, to make some sense out of the tangle in his gut. "Well, what in the hell made ya laugh, then?" he snapped. He neither released his grip nor pulled his face away from Spillman's.

Spillman swallowed visibly and shuddered. "Look," he began, then paused, seeming to realize he didn't know his captor's name, Miss Parsons having only called him "boy." "I swear I never harmed a woman in my life, never molested or even kissed one." A hint of dark humor had come into his voice.

Boy narrowed his gaze. Was this true? Could he trust anything the Jew said? But then, could he trust Leary…or anyone else in Booney? The voice of his mother rang in his ears, telling him to trust no one, to live free. He thought he'd lived by those strange but enticing words all his life, but suddenly he knew he hadn't. All six foot of the dark, heavily muscled man suddenly faced the reality that he'd been nothing more than a dupe. And Spillman knew it. "Still," Boy said slowly, "yer a Jew," unknowingly resorting to a scapegoating as old as Jewish history itself and as senseless.

"True enough," answered Spillman, visibly calming himself as he faced his peril. "I am, as you say, a Jew. But what of it? If I've committed no crime against the women of Booney, then you will beat me—maybe even kill me—simply because I am a Jew?"

Boy released his jaw roughly and began to pace again. "S'pose that's enough to deserve a beatin'," he muttered, unconvincingly.

"Please," Spillman said, in a more gentle voice, "tell me your name. Seems a shame to be beaten by a man I shared a meal with but whose name I don't even know."

"Boy," Boy answered, taking up the cup to get himself a drink of water. "Boy Two-Blood."

If Adam Spillman found the name more bizarre than the situation he found himself in, he did not confess it. "Well then, Boy, shall I tell you something about this Jew?"

Boy filled his cup, drank and put it gently back down on the shelf. He stayed facing away as he nodded.

"There's a reason I came to America, that I wear no beard and eat unkosher chicken."

Boy nodded again, though he didn't understand the relevance of the beard or the strange word he used to describe the chicken. He remembered the taste of the rich, savory flesh with pleasure.

"My people back home call this land golden, say it offers a man the potential to earn great wealth and the freedom to practice our religion without persecution. But it's not that sort of freedom I needed."

The words washed over Boy, strange and incomprehensible to his small worldview. One word, however, stuck. *Freedom.* "A man needs to be free," he said aloud, but mostly to himself.

"Indeed," Spillman answered. "But there are some things a man needs freedom for that can't be found anywhere."

At last, Boy turned. What was the fella getting at? He returned to the chair where the odd-speaking Jew sat so motionless, despite bonds that had to be paining him. In the flickering candlelight, there was a quiet beauty to his face. Boy licked his lips. "What things?" he asked.

Spillman smiled. "Things," he said warmly, "between men."

Boy let out an involuntary groan as his cock began to harden anew, then, catching himself, forced the sound into a growl. He had no word for what Spillman meant, though the people of his town and his country surely did. *Sodomite, pervert, defiler, invert*: so many words with so little understanding. But Boy did understand, and it made his blood boil. He grabbed Spillman and threw him over his shoulder again, then slammed him roughly facedown on his bed. As he slit the ties at his ankles and bound each to the creaky wooden bed frame, his breath through his nostrils was like a bull's and his thoughts were as wild and furious. Yes, he fucked men, but not because he liked it. Or rather he liked it but not because he liked men. His cock was stiffer than he'd ever felt it and aching with need as he bound the Jew. Before he'd even slit Spillman's pants from his body or removed his own, he was panting like a wolf on a bitch in heat.

At last, he mounted his prey, hiking up Spillman's hips as much as the rope allowed and preparing to thrust home with only his copiously leaking cock to ease the way. That Spillman beneath him was making sounds of dismay and struggling did not dissuade him. He'd heard his fill of bawling and begging from every man he'd hunted. He easily thwarted their futile thrashing, and if this one sounded and felt different, it was probably just because he liked it. That thought enraged Boy further, for his fucking was punishment not pleasure. Or if there was pleasure, it was pleasuring for Boy in doing the punishment. Only that. Before plunging inside, he reached down to yank Spillman's head back by his dark, curly hair. "Here's yer freedom," he spat, and thrust home.

Spillman's cries heightened but went unheeded, or perhaps drove Boy on the harder. A Jew was now a man who liked being fucked, and Boy's punishment had to be to make him not like it. He was no longer doing Leary's bidding but his own, teaching a lesson to someone whose crimes had shifted, his evil no longer part of his foreignness but his familiarity. Boy fucked good and

long and hard, gaining leverage from his hand fisted in Spillman's hair and the drive to purge himself of any questions he
still had about what he was doing and why.

When at last he arched and roared out his climax, he collapsed,
sweating and panting, and only then felt the true slackness of
Spillman's body beneath him. The man wasn't unconscious, but
he had given up any attempt at either resistance or pleading. He
wasn't sobbing either, Boy thought with a sureness that pricked
his conscience, what little he had of one. The body beneath him
was warm, the skin smooth, and as he pulled out and left him
lying there, his hand brushed a slender hip that brought a chill
to Boy's hulky frame. He cut the ropes that bound the man and
went to take up his tobacco pouch.

Sitting in the room's one chair that had so recently held
Spillman, Boy rolled himself a cigarette and watched the still
body on his bed, hawk-like. The body hadn't moved, though
Boy could see breathing. He struck a match and inhaled deeply,
the smoke filling his lungs with a familiar, soothing harshness.

When the cigarette was half-finished, Spillman stiffly rolled
to his side with a grunt. His expression was hard to read in the
dim light. Then, in a voice as low and sad as the hills, he said,
"You're no freer than I am."

The words and how the Jew said them struck Boy, at least
enough to drag his chair over and offer Spillman the still-glowing
butt. Spillman accepted, silently, putting a shaking hand on
Boy's as he took it. Boy shuddered. "Why you say I ain't free?"
he asked in an urgent whisper as Spillman inhaled. Boy couldn't
figure why he hadn't said it louder and full of the anger he was
feeling. He was Booney's Hunter, wasn't he? He was the one
who'd done the hunting and the tying and the fucking. He'd
punished the Jew because he wanted to. Well then, wasn't that
freedom?

As if he'd read Boy's mind, Spillman exhaled softly and continued. "Lots of men think freedom is about power, about taking from others, about material gain." He took another drag and handed the butt back to Boy, who took it like it was a hornet and stubbed it out on the floorboards with his bare, calloused heel. "That's not freedom, Boy Two-Blood," came Spillman's powerful low voice.

Boy lifted his head as the stranger whose body he'd just ravaged used his name. He wondered how long it had been since anyone had. He fought back memories of his mother and hated the feeling. This wasn't the time for sentiment. He blinked in the darkness as he watched Spillman blow out smoke and rub his wrists. He drew his tongue across his teeth in thought. "I got my own place," he said, defending himself against what felt like an attack, and one he didn't truly understand. "I do what I like."

Spillman shrugged. "The hunter not the hunted, eh?"

"That's right," Boy said, a little louder now. Maybe they weren't disagreeing after all.

"It's a kind of freedom, I suppose," Spillman acknowledged.

That didn't please Boy a bit. "Best kind," he announced with a nod of his head.

"I know a better kind," said Spillman, his voice strangely gentle and compelling.

"Show me," replied Boy, wanting this secret the Jew had for himself. When Spillman neither moved nor spoke, Boy began to rub his hands on his thighs nervously. His eyes were wide and childlike. "Show me," he repeated, more urgently this time.

Spillman brushed his hair back from his forehead, seeming to consider the request carefully. Then he rose. Boy's jaw dropped. Naked in the dark room, with just the low candlelight burning behind him, the man was mystifying. Slender and willowy, his pale skin nearly glowed, and the black, curling hair that ran from his chest down to his groin shone invitingly. Boy hadn't paid much attention to what the men he hunted looked like undressed. He stripped then fucked them facedown, and when he left them on the roadside, far from town, he didn't spend time considering anything but the job well done and its rewards. As he gaped, he reached to touch his own chest, as hairless as his mother's father, though he couldn't know it. What did the Jew's body hair feel like?

His eyes drifted lower as Spillman took his slender prick into his hand. It thickened at his touch. Boy hadn't spent much time looking at his own cock, but he could tell right off that the Jew's dick was different. Skinless, he might have said. He couldn't imagine what this had to do with freedom, but his eyes were glued to the sight of that hardening, circumcised shaft.

Spillman turned then, not releasing his rigid prize, and patted the bed with his other hand. "Sit down," he invited.

It broke the spell for Boy, those words, and he reacted instinctively, backing away, even though his eyes never left Spillman's body. "Why'd I wanna sit on my bed...with you?"

Spillman smiled and sat down himself. "Because you want to learn about freedom, Boy." The strange cock stayed hard even as Spillman let it go.

The use of his name again did the trick, and an enthralled Boy Two-Blood stepped forward to sit beside the Jew who clearly knew secrets and was going to share them.

The moment he sat, Spillman's head was facedown in Boy's lap, lips around his shaft and sucking him. Boy lacked any reference for such an act. He could guess some people did such things, but no one had ever done them to Boy. The sensation was incredible and he was quickly so hard he ached. He could only look dumbly on, fingers outstretched but not touching the Jew as he was expertly handled, sucked and stroked and laid back on his filthy bed without even noticing he'd shifted positions.

Even if he were given to careful thought and glib tongue, Boy would not have been able to say how Spillman made him so passive and pliant. There was a bare moment's pause and, panting like a dog, Boy opened his tight-shut eyes to see the cocksucker had risen and nimbly made his way to the stove. It looked like he was thinking about dipping his hand in the can of bacon grease, then shaking his head and turning away, then going back and doing it. The strange vision was confirmed when Spillman returned smelling of pig, his pale, hard prick glistening with grease. Boy was enthralled at the strange sight; and whether it was disbelief or a profound trust born in desperation for the secret to freedom Spillman held in that cock and his dark, mischievous eyes, Boy willingly spread his thick-muscled thighs when the Jew demanded he do so.

If no one had ever sucked Boy Two-Blood's prick, there was even less doubt that no one had ever tried to fuck him. Spillman's words came like an incantation. "Easy now," he cooed, as if Boy was a stallion ready to bolt. Perhaps he was. The Jew nudged his slippery, circumcised head into the dark cleft, and Boy began to shake. But he did not throw him off. "That's right, nice and easy. Oh yes. Adam's going to bring you back to yourself, Boy. He's going to show you freedom." The voice was melodic, exotic, the words an entrancing lullaby that kept the huge mountain man still as he was entered by Adam, named for the first man on earth, while a firm hand returned to stroke Boy's flagging erection back to hardness.

The sounds that came from Boy's throat then had probably never been heard before: low, needful, animal sounds. Spillman fed the beast deeply, tipping Boy's hips back until the timbre of his moans lost their edge of fear and shifted into pleasure. "Feel that," Spillman enthused, "that place inside that's never been touched before." His voice was rougher now, thick with desire. He began to thrust harder. Boy cried out, neither knowing nor caring whether it was in pleasure or pain, his body surrendering to Spillman's fuck, arching and bucking with increasing abandon.

Boy began to sweat and to shake. Spillman was driving into him with speed and force that sang through Boy's every nerve and fiber. Though his cock was half the size of Boy's, that slick little cobra knew exactly how to strike. Over and over, Boy felt the pounding inside him, that place Spillman spoke of nudged and rubbed with a rhythm that matched his racing pulse and the throb in his leaking cock. With a sudden clarity, Boy knew himself as neither hunter nor hunted, neither cut off nor controlled by others. As every muscle in his body tensed in preparation for a climax that threatened to be both physically and emotionally more powerful than anything he'd known before, he looked deeply into Adam Spillman's eyes, where he saw freedom. Spillman's head tipped back, exposing his tender throat, and Boy's hand went up to grip it instinctually. Boy's roar met Spillman's ecstatically choked cry of release as both men peaked with a simultaneity that, for Boy, proved the magic of Spillman's promise beyond the slightest doubt.

Boy released the slender, vulnerable throat as Spillman collapsed on top of him. A shaggy head on his chest was as new a sensation as being fucked, but his hand rose to stroke the sweaty mop of hair as naturally as he'd spread his legs. As he felt Adam Spillman's heart beating against his, he knew he was truly free.

The love of gossip vied with baffled silence as folks tried to make sense of what had happened that night between Boy and the

Jew to end instantly and forever the career of Booney's Hunter. When Spillman returned to town the next week with a bundle of Boy's pelts and hides to trade, people were aghast, especially when he'd traded for three live chickens and a rooster. Whether Spillman was Boy Two-Blood's servant or roommate or lover, no one dared ask. "Live and let live," the townsfolk said, unsure how else to react. "Live free," Boy and Adam answered.

# JOHNNY
# AND CLYDE

## K. Vale

John Baros held up two fingers, and the bleach-blond bartender with the bright-orange tan poured him another double of Jack. He needed a little more liquid courage before he cleaned out his bank account and skipped town.

*God, how had it come to this?*

His career had been ripe with promise. The bigwigs at Friedman and Lansky had been grooming him for greatness— or so they had made him believe. And then the IRS started sniffing around. The boatloads of accounting work he had done for F&L, LLP suddenly took on a suspicious gleam. He had stayed at the office long after midnight, digging up damning evidence and chewing his fingernails down to raw skin. It wasn't just the ship that would sink for the phony numbers. He would drown along with it. The scariest part was not the potential prison sentence, but the fact that the boys at F&L didn't appreciate rust spots in their armor. They likely had been grooming him, but to be their fall guy rather than their next CEO. John doubted he would make it to court to testify against them, even if the Feds were kind enough to cut him a deal.

Well, he refused to try to save himself legitimately. Yes, it would make him appear guilty, but better falsely accused than dead. He had socked away a decent chunk of change over the past three years. He lived in a tiny apartment that cost a fraction of his salary. He had no ties here, not since he and Michael had broken up. And there was his grandparents' home in Greece to consider. All he had to do was get his money. The plane ticket was already purchased.

He was shaking as he raised the amber liquid to his lips. What if the Feds were there waiting for him at the bank; anticipating his every move like on television? Even scarier, what if the Kosher Nostra got word of his imminent bugout?

He brought the glass back to his coaster and glanced at the booth in the corner of the pub. A man was speaking with the waitress, ordering another beer by the looks of it. He was gorgeous. John stared, unable to pull his eyes away. A knuckle tattoo marched starkly across the guy's left hand. Squinting as inconspicuously as possible, John tried to make out the letters. *Damn.* If he weren't planning to disappear by the end of the day, and if the rugged guy didn't seem so far out of his league, John would consider buying him the drink.

John glanced down at his own pristine suit and tie and then back at the man. Black biker boots decked out with a row of metal rings caught his eye, and he slid his gaze up thick, jean-clad legs. Black T-shirt, black leather jacket, and a dark circle-beard that pointed at the chin completed his sinister getup. The man looked tall and was certainly broader of shoulder than John. *Fuck*, he was a sucker for a big guy. Biker Boy's head was shaved to a glistening sheen, but his eyebrows were thick, dark and crouched low over piercing, blue eyes as he warily scanned his surroundings. John wondered if he was waiting for someone.

A minute or two later, another man approached and slid into the seat across from the fierce-looking stud.

*That settles that. No delaying your trip for a quick fuck, Johnny.*

John paid his tab and slunk out into the sunlight.

"Don't fuckin' move. I got a gun on yer back." *Was that an Irish or a Scottish accent?*

The hoarse voice that whispered in John's ear inexplicably caused a surge of blood to his cock, even as a muscular arm was slung around his neck and the muzzle of a gun jabbed into his rib cage.

*What the fuck?* He had just finished removing every penny from his account. The astonished teller had needed to be convinced he was putting a cash deposit on a short-sale house, but she finally handed over the money. Johnny had stuffed it in his messenger bag with a sigh of relief. He was walking out to freedom, and still imagining the hotty from the bar coming all over his chest, when the madness began.

Three guys with ski masks covering their faces rushed in. One had grabbed him in a headlock before he could even process what was happening. The other two made short work with the tellers, urging them with sweeping pistols to pack all of their cash into cloth sacks with astonishing speed.

"No cops—or the hostage gets it!" The man behind him growled. *Definitely Scottish.* The patrons had all plastered themselves to the floor. The tellers scrambled to obey. No one was going to be a hero, here. John moved when the robber moved. The distant sound of sirens pierced the glass walls of the bank, and the three criminals moved out. John was dragged along.

"Collateral." The man spoke against his ear, and John got harder.

"Ye tell the cops, we got a hostage!" he shouted at the stunned-silent spectators as he pulled John out the door.

The wailing grew louder and the bandits raced down an alley with John in tow. He didn't resist. Didn't scan his surroundings for a chance to break free. For some insane reason, he felt as if he were running toward liberty. Had his life become such a fucked-up mess, that this surreal episode seemed like…fun?

Three motorcycles were pulled from behind a dumpster. The men hastily threw their booty into zippered bags mounted on the tanks of all three bikes.

"Get on!" The man barked at John from his seat on one bike. The gun was trained on his face, but John stared into the electric-blue eyes behind the mask and didn't feel a shred of fear. He swung a leg over and wrapped his arms around the bigger man's waist. Engines revved and the chase was on.

John knew he was only on the bike to keep the thieves from being shot at. He knew he should be rooting for the police who zigged and zagged down narrow side streets as they tried to keep pace with the wildly maneuvering bikes. He knew he shouldn't enjoy the sensation of his cock and balls snugged up against the backside of the man in front of him, especially since he preferred to bottom. But he sighed with relief when the sirens grew fainter. And he groaned as his hard-on was rubbed provocatively with each turn of the handlebars.

Maybe it was only his imagination, but it seemed like the ass in front of him was more active than the leaning bike demanded.

The three bikers split up, and John found himself flying down a dirt lane at breakneck speed, his arms tightly hugging the dangerous stranger in front of him. Wind whipped his face, stung his eyes to a liquid blur. The green-brown of forest sailed by in smudged watercolor. The grim reaper could have loomed alongside the lonely stretch of road, and John would have reached out a hand to high-five him.

When they finally skidded to a stop at the rear of a small cabin somewhere in the lonely woods of upstate New York, or possibly even Vermont, John had an aching hard on, a wind-slapped face and the sweetest sense of abandon. It didn't matter that the masked guy still had a gun tucked in his pants. John had noticed the tattooed message on the biker's fingers as the man had choked the throttle. The right-hand knuckles, deciphered from John's upside-down vantage point, read OUTS. The left was inked with IDER. *Outsider.* The word called to him. It made him believe that he and the rough biker were somehow meant to be here right now. They were like the cogs in a clock that gripped together perfectly to push each other forward.

The man slid off the bike. He faced John as he pulled the pistol from the front of his pants. Johnny could only stare at the smattering of dark belly hair that led down into his jeans. He licked his lips and imagined tracing the angry red welt left by the hard metal barrel. With his mouth watering, he devoured the guy's semi-aroused state with his eyes. The gun wasn't trained on him, but held at the robber's side. Even so, John didn't feel that approaching the guy was a wise move.

Instead, he inched a hand over his own hard dick and slid it down his bound length then back up, wrapping his fingers around himself as much as the dress slacks allowed, and stroking. The man watched him silently.

"Let me taste your cock," John said gruffly, still unsure if his words would get him killed. How did he know this guy wasn't ramrod straight and homophobic as well? He saw the hint of a pink tongue dart out to wet the man's lips under the knit mask, and blood surged to his prick, full and fast and almost painful.

The man was unbuckling his belt. Unbuttoning. Unzipping.

"Come 'ere."

John knelt on the hard ground before a pair of black boots decorated with steel rings.

That first taste of precome made his own cock drip. He worked his tongue against the guy's slit, hungry for more, before he slicked a wet tongue down the veined length. With one fist, John grasped the base as he pulled the fat head into his mouth. His other hand fumbled with the fly on his suit pants, working his raging-hard dick out. He ran a thumb over his wet tip and used the moisture to jerk lightly just under his head, on the tender cord of frenulum, while he swallowed the guy's entire length in noisy gulps.

Head bobbing up and down, Johnny felt the prick in his mouth grow wider; felt one hand weave firm fingers through his hair while the cold weight of a pistol rubbed his scalp from the other side. The guy made throaty humming sounds above him, and John had to freeze the hand on his own dick before he shot too soon.

"Fuck. Fine head," the man grunted in his thick brogue. He pulled back on Johnny's hair, yanking his mouth off.

"Yer looking to get fucked, boy? Want me to stick this cock in yer ass?"

John could only nod. The guy unlocked the cabin door and jerked his covered head toward it in silent command. John obeyed.

The shack was small, dusty. A tiny kitchen opened to the living space. Shabby couch, beat-up coffee table and card table with three rusty chairs completed the décor.

"Pull out that couch," Blue Eyes commanded, as he rested the gun on the poker table.

John tugged it open while sparing frequent glances at the man. The Scot fondled his dick while he watched John work.

"Don't think ye need the suit fer this," he growled, once the bare mattress was exposed. John pulled off his clothes with trembling fingers. The guy kicked off his boots and shrugged out of his jacket, but didn't seem inclined to do more. He only rubbed his hard-on through the gaping V of his unzipped jeans and yanked down briefs. John pulled the messenger bag from his neck and dropped it to the floor. His clothes followed in a hasty pile.

He swallowed and approached the thief. Brushing hands with the man, he wrapped his fingers around his hard length. John stretched up to stick his tongue in the mouth hole of the mask. The man met him with a hot, wet kiss. Soft acrylic pulled against the slight stubble on John's cheeks and chin. He imagined how the facial hair under the knit would feel against his lips. His dick. Tickling his spread ass.

The bank robber groaned into his mouth and then pushed John away.

"Spit on my cock before I put it in ya," he demanded, pushing down on John's shoulders. He fell to his knees eagerly as his mouth worked up a ball of saliva. John spat, and worked the lube against the man's head with his fist. All the while, he watched those blue eyes fixed on him.

"Lay down. Wanna watch ye jerk off while I'm inside."

John sprawled out on the lumpy mattress. Springs poked his back and he didn't care. *Condom!* Common sense tried to intervene, but that strange sense of freedom overruled safety. He didn't have a rubber on him, and he knew without asking the other man didn't either.

The biker stroked his uncut cock as he sank to his knees before John. He grasped the base in a choke hold and pressed his bulging red head against John's hole. John was mesmerized by the sight of him: black mask with the hint of a glistening tongue poking out of the slit, and bright turquoise eyes that watched with rapt attention as John massaged his own dick.

The man probed against his asshole with agonizing gentleness. John's balls were already tugged up tight with need. He wanted to scream for the man to fuck him, but he held back, slowed his hand and wiggled closer to his tormenter.

And then, in a single thrust, the masked man pushed past the tight ring and pumped fully into him. His nuts clapped against John's ass as John let out an alarmed grunt. The man stilled, watching John with his intense gaze.

The immediate fullness forced all the air from his lungs. He didn't feel capable of inhaling for a few heartbeats. He sucked in a cautious breath and released it. And then the man eased back out of him. Slowly back in. John's hand slid down his own shaft in response. The initial sting faded as the spit-slick cock pumped between his cheeks. He'd never been fucked by a man with a foreskin before. It was unbelievably smooth. The extra skin rolled forward and back in a fluid motion that made the penetration deliciously sleek.

John pressed his hips and groaned each time the guy's head bumped his front wall.

"So fuckin' tight, boy," the guy whispered as he surged into him. "Don't ya come yet. I want to shoot all over yer pretty cock."

John squeezed his eyes closed and bit his lower lip. *Don't come yet. Don't come yet.*

The dick in his ass pulled out, and a warm, wet blast pulsed over his prick, drizzled down his balls. He had to still his hand to keep from spurting himself. He waited for permission while every cell in his body screeched for release.

And then his cockhead was pulled into hot suction, and he inhaled sharply. His eyes flew open. His dick was lost in the mouth hole of the mask as the bank robber deep-throated him. The guy's come streaked white across the black knit. He locked eyes with John as he bobbed shallow, and then deep, to suck his own juice off John's erection. The sight of his dick disappearing into the black slit was entrancing; there was something so impersonal and yet so intimate about it. *So fucking erotic, like a glory hole with beautiful blue eyes.*

The tension in John's balls burst with a nearly painful twinge. His abdomen convulsed with shock waves as he climaxed in the guy's mouth. The pleasure-pulses ebbed. John shivered while the man sucked every last drop from him before finally backing off.

The masked man slid up next to him and wrapped John against his burly chest. Together they fell asleep.

Dawn crept with blue-gray fingers through the tattered curtains. John rolled over and rubbed his eyes. The mystery man was nowhere to be seen, but a strip of light shone beneath a door that came off the tiny kitchen. The sounds of a shower reached him as he rolled off the uncomfortable mattress.

The biker's jacket was draped over the back of a chair and John slid his hands into the soft leather pockets. He pulled out a paper-stuffed wallet that was bound with a rubber band. With trembling hands he undid the fold. Inside he found a passport with the name Duncan Clyde ascribed to the fierce man in the picture. One look at that scowl made John's pulse speed up. He rewrapped the wallet and slid it back inside.

In his own wallet, John found an old receipt. A pen was in the side pouch of his messenger bag. He scrawled his cell phone number, and the address to his family's home in Volos, Greece, on the back of the paper. He considered adding his name, but instead signed it, *Another Outsider,* before he slid it into the thief's jacket pocket. He heard the water turn off and crept back to the couch. When the door opened quietly, he held his eyes closed. Footsteps stopped at the end of the makeshift bed and remained unmoving for an excruciating length of time.

What was the man thinking as he stared at his sleeping hostage? John fought the urge to open his eyes, stretch, fake a groggy wake-up. The boots moved on, toward the man's jacket. A soft whisper of fabric sliding over arms ended with a zip. And then he walked out. The motorcycle roared to life. John watched from the corner of a window as the dust from the bike's trail settled in its wake. Within minutes, the far-off sounds of the engine had faded to deafening silence.

John slung his bag across his chest and walked out into the early morning. He pulled his phone out to check for cell service and wasn't surprised to find none. He turned west and began the long walk toward civilization. He had his memories of last night to keep him company all the way there.

# HELLFIRE

## Wayne Mansfield

Taylor took one last drag on his cigarette and tossed it to the ground, where it lay smoking by the feet of someone behind him in the long queue. "Fuck, I hate standing outside a club waiting to get in," he said.

His friend Ryan, a tall, lean, muscular twenty-nine-year-old, agreed. "Especially in this part of town. I mean, shit, get a load of those bouncers. They look like they'd roll you for five bucks and a smoke."

Taylor gave the two bouncers the once-over. Both were built like brick shithouses and had heads that were shiny domes of tanned skin. The one nearest Taylor was the better looking of the two, although he wouldn't mind being fucked by either one of them. But the one on the left had piercing blue eyes rimmed by thick, black lashes. He also had a dark moustache and goatee. Taylor could also make out the top of a tattoo on his neck, just above the line of the collar he wore. Farther down, below the thick leather belt, there was a world-class bulge and Taylor wondered if the bouncer wasn't just a little erect.

"If we don't get in soon, I reckon we should go to Trash. You never have to line up there," said Ryan, glancing at his watch.

Taylor nodded. "I hope we don't have to, though. I've heard good things about this club."

Hellfire was an alternative club and accordingly the people in the queue were an eclectic mix of bikers, goths, punks and wannabe vampires. It wasn't a gay club, but the word around town was that a guy could get himself a nice bit of biker cock there or get his arse blasted with a load of punk cum if he played his cards right. Or he could get bashed within an inch of his life if he played them wrong. The anticipation of the former sorts of encounters meant it was going to take a lot to force Taylor from his place in the slowly advancing queue.

Finally he and Ryan made it to the front of the line. Taylor, who'd been itching to get a closer look at the two bouncers, especially the one with the blue eyes, bowed his head and started checking out the thick pole hanging to the left in the blue-eyed bouncer's black trousers. Just imagining what such a massive cock would look like soon had his own cock stiffening. The problem was, unlike the bouncer's trousers, his jeans were skintight and even a slight increase in size was immediately noticeable. He looked from the bouncer's bulge to his own and then back at the bouncer's. Then he looked up to discover the bouncer staring at him; a dark crease between his eyebrows.

Taylor felt his face flush. He didn't know where to look.

Fortunately, just at that moment, a goth girl with black lips and bright-pink dreadlocks came tottering out of the club on gravity-defying heels.

"Seeya later, Bruce," she said to the bouncer on the right.

She kissed him on the cheek, leaving a faint gray mark on his lightly tanned skin. "'Night, Terry."

*Terry.* Taylor made a mental note of the name.

"All right," said Bruce, nodding at Ryan. "*You* can go in."

"We're together," said Ryan, pointing to Taylor with his thumb.

"How nice for ya," grunted the bouncer. "Ya goin' in or what?"

"Can he come in with me?"

"One out, one in. Now get in before I change me mind."

The blue-eyed bouncer folded his arms and looked menacingly at Ryan.

"Go in, mate," said Taylor. "I'll meet you up there in a minute."

"You sure?"

Bouncer Bruce folded his arms across his chest and sighed impatiently. The frown line on his forehead deepened.

"Yeah. Quickly." Taylor gave his friend a gentle push and Ryan disappeared into the darkness on the other side of the door.

Taylor gave Terry, the blue-eyed bouncer, a nervous smile. "Sorry about that," he said. "It's our first time here."

The information had no visible effect on either of the bouncers, both of whom had now unfolded their arms. Bruce lit up a cigarette and looked up the street as he exhaled a cloud of dirty, gray smoke.

After what seemed like an eternity two more goth girls stumbled out of the darkness and onto the neon-lit footpath. Giggling, they staggered arm in arm to the fast-food café next door and went in.

"All right, you two," said Bruce pointing to the punk couple standing directly behind Taylor.

"Hey, I was next," he protested.

"But there's only one of you and there's two of them," Bruce explained.

The punk couple, with matching studded collars, pushed past Taylor and disappeared into Hellfire.

Taylor caught Bruce winking at Terry. They were both smirking, which made Taylor's blood start to boil.

When a large biker with a handlebar moustache and tatty leather jacket barged out through the door, Taylor was confident he'd be next. One person out, one person in. He took a step forward.

"You," said Bruce, pointing to someone who wasn't Taylor.

"That's it," snapped Taylor, who was now too pissed off to care that both bouncers were at least twice his size. "I'm going in."

He managed two steps before Terry pushed the palm of his hand against Taylor's chest.

"Ya lookin' for trouble?" Terry growled.

Taylor felt someone push past him into the club. "No," he said. "It's just my friend's in there waiting for me."

"That's too bad then, ain't it?"

Taylor's whole body tensed. He could feel his hands balling themselves into fists. Even before he did it, he knew he was making a mistake.

"I'm going in," he repeated in a more determined tone.

He sidestepped Terry's extended hand and shouldered his way past the bouncer. He managed one step before he felt two powerful arms grab him by the shoulders.

"Right, dickhead. Ya comin' with me. Look after the door, Bruce." With his massive hands gripping Taylor's shoulders, Terry marched Taylor toward the side of the building.

"What are you doing?" snarled Taylor. "Get your fucking hands off me. Where are you taking me?"

Taylor was furious, but amidst the burning anger, there was fear. He knew he was good looking. When other friends talked about what they would change if they could afford plastic surgery, he could never think of anything he'd like to change. Now he was in danger of the bouncer doing some facial rear-rangement for free.

"Mate, I'm sorry. I'll leave. I don't want any trouble."

The narrow alleyway between Hellfire and the fast-food café was quite well lit near the street, but was pitch-black farther down.

In silence Terry pushed Taylor into the darkness, which wasn't as complete as it had looked from the street. In fact, once Taylor's eyes had adjusted to the lack of light, he could see the bouncer quite clearly.

His heart was racing. Adrenaline had flooded his veins. He tried to swallow and found that his throat had become so dry that he could barely feel his tongue.

Terry released him. He took a couple of steps backward. "Listen, man. I'm really sorry I gave you any trouble."

He saw the dark shape of Terry's arm lifting into the air. He saw Terry draw his arm back before it flashed forward. Thwack! Suddenly Taylor felt himself flying through the air. He couldn't breathe. The bouncer had winded him. He crashed against the wall and fell to the litter-strewn ground clutching his stomach.

"I don't like people makin' me job difficult," Terry growled.

Taylor wanted to respond, to apologize once more, but he was struggling to catch his breath. *At least it wasn't in the face,* he thought, before the realization dawned on him that perhaps the bouncer wasn't finished with him yet.

"Sorry," he managed to say, the last syllable catching in his throat and making him cough.

He felt the bouncer grab his head. He closed his eyes and

waited for the impact of the man's fist. Instead he felt something more familiar.

"Suck it, ya little fag," said Terry, sliding the smooth head of his erect cock back and forth across Taylor's lips.

Taylor took the head of the cock into his mouth. If this was all he had to do to atone for whatever sin he had committed against the bouncer, then he was getting off very lightly.

Terry's cock was long and thick, but with a relatively small head. Already he could taste the sweet honey of the man's precum. As his tongue slid around and around the head of the cock, he couldn't help but dip the tip of his tongue into the man's piss-slit to gather a small bead of man-nectar to swallow down.

"Stop fuckin' around," growled Terry, grabbing a handful of Taylor's hair. "Suck it like a bitch!"

Taylor's head was pulled back and forth, so that his mouth slid up and down Terry's erect shaft. He opened up his throat to accommodate the thick girth and closed his eyes to concentrate on not gagging. He grabbed the base of Terry's cock and regained some control over how fast and deep he went. After a dozen or so attempts, he was able to get the whole cock in his mouth and in no time at all he could feel the cockhead pushing against the very back of his throat. His cocksucking seemed to please Terry, who had released his tight grip on Taylor's hair and was now only gently pulling on it.

More and more precum dribbled out of the man's cock. The taste of it filled Taylor's mouth. And when the thick prick was right down his throat and Taylor's nose was buried in the bouncer's thick bush, he could smell the sweat and piss of unwashed pubic hair. The aroma turned him on and made his cock twitch each time the heady scent filled his nostrils.

Then, without warning, Terry withdrew his cock and turned around.

"Eat me arse," he said.

Taylor placed a hand on each of Terry's large, meaty arsecheeks and pulled them apart. As he leaned in he could smell the musty man-stink of an unwashed hole. He closed his eyes and leaned in a little farther, but then balked.

"Eat it," growled Terry, reaching around and cupping a large hand on the back of Taylor's head.

Suddenly Taylor felt his face being pulled into the crevice between the twin mounds of Terry's buttcheeks. The tip of his nose disappeared into the man's arsehole. The smell was overpowering, but not as unpleasant as he'd first thought. There was a thick ring of hair around the puckered chute, which tickled the freshly shaved skin around his lips. Those hairs, which had trapped the accumulated smells of shit, sweat and pheromone, were undoubtedly the source of the manly perfume.

He removed his nose from Terry's hole and replaced it with his tongue. At first he circled the puckered flesh with the tip of his tongue, licking around and around. Then he started stabbing at the hole with a tongue made firm by contracting the muscle. He pulled the arsecheeks farther apart and pushed his face farther in. The tip of his tongue disappeared through the band of muscle, eliciting from Terry a small moan of pleasure.

He continued to tongue-fuck the bouncer's hole, interrupting the action by rubbing his face over the hole and covering himself in the man's arse smell. Then he would go back to stabbing at the hole with his tongue. He tried to get his tongue deeper and deeper in with each thrust, and when it was inside he would try and wriggle the tip. Invariably this tongue tickling would draw a small moan from Terry, who had started gyrating slowly against Taylor's face.

When he'd had enough, the bouncer stood up and let his

pants drop to a crumpled heap around his ankles.

"Take ya clothes off," he said.

Taylor scrambled to his feet. "All of them?"

"Yeah. All of 'em," replied the bouncer.

"Why?" asked Taylor. "Why not just my jeans?"

"Coz I said so, that's why," growled the bouncer.

Reluctantly Taylor took his shoes and socks off and then slid his jeans and underpants off. Finally he removed his jacket and T-shirt.

A slight breeze against the bare flesh of his slim, toned and hairless body made him shiver. He brought his arms up and crossed them over his chest to block the effects of the late-night breeze.

"Up against the wall," said Terry.

Taylor did as he was told.

"Turn around," said the bouncer, shuffling up close to him.

Taylor glanced down at Terry's thick cock jutting up into the air and turned around. Part of him was excited at the prospect of having something so long and thick penetrate him, but not even the copious amounts of pre-ooze the bouncer's cock was producing seemed enough to make penetration any less uncomfortable.

Terry went down on his knees and Taylor felt the man's tongue licking his arsehole. He arched his back and thrust his smooth arse out at the randy bouncer. He felt Terry grab his toned arsecheeks and yank them apart. Soon Terry was sucking and slurping at Taylor's hole, licking and poking at the pucker and making some incredible sounds while he was at it.

Taylor's cock twitched as the bristles of the bouncer's top lip and jaw scratched against the sensitive skin around his arsehole.

"That feels so good," he heard himself moan.

"This is gonna feel better," Terry replied.

Taylor felt the head of the bouncer's cock press against his arsehole, which was slick with saliva and precum. A finger massaged the slippery concoction over the puckers and into the entrance to his arsehole, preparing him for penetration.

"Ya ready?"

Taylor was surprised the bouncer had even bothered to ask. He'd previously been so rough, so keen to satisfy his own pleasures, that his question took Taylor by surprise.

"Yes," he replied and he immediately felt the head of Terry's cock being slowly pushed through the tight ring of muscle.

Taylor felt his arse being invaded by the bouncer's massive prick in gradual increments. It felt like he was being penetrated by a cannon rather than a man's cock.

Terry's hands gripped his hips and when the entire length of veined cock was inside him, Terry began to thrust.

At first there were gentle thrusts. Taylor was grateful. Even though it felt good to feel something so thick inside him, there was still a little discomfort. When his arse muscles had become accustomed to Terry's cock and had relaxed he felt the bouncer begin to thrust a little harder and faster.

Terry continued thrusting as one arm wrapped around Taylor's chest, drawing his body back against his own, while the fingers of the other hand wrapped themselves around Taylor's cock.

"How's that feel, fag?"

Terry's breathe on his neck and his whispered growl sent tingles spilling down the bones of Taylor's spine.

"Feels good," was all he could manage to say.

Terry's hips remained busy, plunging his cock into Taylor's hole before pulling back in readiness to plunge in yet again. Simultaneously, his arm pulled down on Taylor's torso for maximum penetration. Each thrust produced a sharp exhalation from Taylor. Terry's hand pulled his head back so their lips could meet. They kissed. It was hard keeping their lips together. Each time Terry thrust, their mouths were dislodged, though somehow their tongues always remained touching, staying in contact until their lips could find each other again.

At one stage Taylor realized that Terry was doing all the work. Terry was fucking his hole, jerking him off and kissing his lips. He felt like a sex toy that existed solely for Terry's pleasure. He didn't mind one bit. In fact, apart from a terrifying start, this was the most exciting fuck he'd ever had.

Their kisses grew more and more passionate. Bursts of warm breath exploded into Taylor's mouth. He breathed them in as Terry's hips bucked faster and harder up into him. Combined with Terry's firm hand on his cock, jerking him off, and Terry's lips on his, Taylor knew it wouldn't be long before he was spraying his load all over the brick wall in front of him.

"I'm getting close," he panted.

"Are ya, ya little bitch?" growled Terry. "Ya gettin' ready to blow, are ya?"

With each word Terry stabbed his prick deeper and harder into Taylor. A couple of times the power of his thrusts made Taylor wince. His arse had become accustomed to Terry's thick cock, but it was filled to capacity so any sudden movements had the effect of making his eyes water.

Then Taylor felt fingers at his nipples, pinching them and twisting them. He leaned back against Terry's shoulder and a long groan emanated from his throat.

"Ya like me pinchin' ya tits, bitch?"

Taylor couldn't answer. His abdominal muscles were contracting. He could feel his cock swelling. He began breathing erratically as a familiar sensation welled in his groin. He felt his arse muscles clamping down on Terry's thick cock, accentuating the sensation of the man-sized muscle plowing into him.

When he came, he felt as if a tidal wave of pure ecstasy was washing over him. He shuddered and shook beneath Terry's arms as a thick stream of cum splattered against the bricks in front. A surprising amount of pearly white paste shot out of Taylor's cock, far more than he could ever remember having shot before, and just as the last remnant of cum dribbled out of his cock he heard Terry grunt.

Terry's hands dropped to Taylor's waist, where they gripped him, pulling his arse back to meet his thrusts with a force that rocked Taylor's whole body. He didn't mind. Knowing that his arse was being seeded by the burly bouncer made everything okay, and when he got home later that night he'd enjoy jerking off again while fingering his cum-soaked arsehole.

Taylor felt the bouncer's body relax. It was all over. What he thought was going to be the bashing of his life had turned into the fuck of his life. At least the best fuck he'd had up to that moment.

Terry released his grip. "Turn around."

Taylor did as the bouncer asked him and soon as he was facing Terry. The man put his hands on Taylor's shoulders and forced him onto his knees.

"Suck it," said the bouncer.

"What?" asked Taylor, not sure he'd heard correctly.

"Just get ya mouth on there," Terry snarled, slapping Taylor's face before pulling it up against the still-hard cock that had just been buried to the hilt inside his arsehole.

Taylor reached up and gripped the base of Terry's cock before guiding the head into his mouth. He licked around the head, then took the rest of the cock down his throat until his nose was pressed into the flesh beneath the bouncer's pubes.

"That's it, fag," said Terry holding Taylor's head down. "Suck me dirty cock. Clean it up real good."

Taylor could feel his face going red. He tried to bring his head back, but the bouncer was too strong. He gagged and coughed, though the cough got caught in his throat and he gagged again. Just when he thought he would pass out, the bouncer released him.

"Now suck my nuts." Taylor felt the sharp sting of another slap, this time to the other side of his face. "Suck those big balls."

Taylor began by licking the hairy sac then took one massive nut into his mouth and sucked on it.

"Ah that's it, fag. Suck those big boys."

Taylor released one then sucked the other one into his mouth. After running his tongue over and around the rubbery gonad, he stretched his mouth open wide and sucked the second nut into his mouth.

"Fuck that feels good," Terry moaned.

Taylor glanced up and saw the bouncer's head fall back against his shoulders. He continued sucking although it was difficult with two sizeable balls in his mouth.

Terry patted him on the head. "Good little doggy," he said. "Now lick me hole again."

Taylor felt a small frown materialize on his face. He was getting a bit sick of this game. They'd both cum and, after all, Terry was supposed to be working. Despite the warm glow around his arsehole, he wondered when it would all end.

Terry burst out laughing. "Now put ya clothes back on and I'll let ya in to find ya little fag friend."

Taylor wiped his mouth and nose on the back of his arm then squatted down. He patted the ground in the area where he had dropped his clothing and soon found the small pile of fabric and leather. As quickly as he could he dressed himself. The bouncer was already walking back toward the street; his footsteps were growing fainter and fainter. He hurriedly pulled on his shirt and jacket and then his underpants, the wrong way around, and finally his jeans, socks and shoes.

He began to walk quickly toward the lights and noise of the nearby street with a slight squelching sensation in the crevice between his arsecheeks. It made him smile, remembering that he had an arse full of the bouncer's cum. *Wait til I tell Ryan*, he thought as he stepped into the brightly lit street.

He approached the entrance to Hellfire with a sense of trepidation. His eyes were riveted on Terry, who had just finished saying something to Bruce. He steeled himself for humiliation. It would be just like Terry to tell him to fuck off, even after what he'd done to him.

Suddenly he was standing at the front of the queue, with angry eyes from those waiting to go in upon him.

"Hey buddy, there's a line here. Get to the back of it," said a muscular man with tattoos all up and down his bare arms.

"Yeah, piss off to the back of the line," said a long-haired girl hanging off his arm.

"Hey, you!"

Taylor turned.

It was Bruce. "Get to the back—"

Terry cut in. "Nah, he's good to go." Terry gave his head a flick. "Go on. Get in there."

Taylor smiled weakly and kept his eyes on his shoes to avoid any eye contact. He hurried past the two bouncers and into the club. *How long have I been in the alley?* he wondered. *I bloody-well hope Ryan hasn't gone home and left me here.*

# ABOUT THE EDITOR AND AUTHORS

**SHANE ALLISON**'s editing career began with the publication of his best-selling gay erotic anthology *Hot Cops: Gay Erotic Stories*, which was one of his proudest moments. He has since gone on to publish over a dozen gay erotica anthologies such as *Straight Guys: Gay Erotic Fantasies*, *Cruising: Gay Erotic Stories*, *Middle Men: Gay Erotic Threesomes*, *Frat Boys: Gay Erotic Stories*, *Brief Encounters: 69 Hot Gay Shorts*, *College Boys: Gay Erotic Stories*, *Hardworking Men: Gay Erotic Fiction*, *Hot Cops: Gay Erotic Fiction*, *Backdraft: Fireman Erotica* and *Afternoon Pleasures: Erotica for Gay Couples*. Shane Allison has appeared in five editions *of Best Gay Erotica*, *Best Black Gay Erotica* and *Zane's Z-Rated: Chocolate Flava 3*. His debut poetry collection, *Slut Machine* is out from Queer Mojo and his poem/memoir *I Remember* is out from Future Tense Books. Shane is at work on a novel and currently resides in Tallahassee, Florida.

**MICHAEL BRACKEN's** short fiction has been published in *Best Gay Romance 2010, Beautiful Boys, Biker Boys, Black Fire, Boy Fun, Boys Getting Ahead, Country Boys, Freshmen, The Handsome Prince, Homo Thugs, Hot Blood, The Mammoth Book of Best New Erotica 4, Men, Muscle Men, Teammates* and other anthologies and periodicals.

**MARTHA DAVIS** is an Atlanta-based writer of erotica, erotic romance and M/M fiction. She has been seen recently lurking around the pages of the Ravenous Romance anthology *Spankalicious: Erotic Adventures in Spanking*. Find her at facebook.com/quixoticorchid.

**LANDON DIXON's** writing credits include stories in the anthologies *Straight? Volume 2, Friction 7, Working Stiff, Brief Encounters, Hot Daddies, Hot Jocks, Uniforms Unzipped, Black Dungeon Masters, Ultimate Gay Erotica* and *Best Gay Erotica*; and short story collections *Hot Tales of Gay Lust* and *Hot Tales of Gay Lust 2*.

**WES HARTLEY** is blue-collar-boy-curious. His ongoing up-close-and-personal hands-on research into the same-sexual gamesmanship of dangerous hardhat boys have been personally rewarding. He's written twenty-two books and numberless stories, poems and essays. His most recent book is *The Kisses of Boys*. Wes lives near world-famous Kitsilano Beach in Vancouver, Canada.

**REGINALD T. JACKSON** (ReginaldTJackson.com) is a founding member of Other Countries: Black Gay Men Writing Collective, author of the poetry volumes *Hejira: From Cradle To Grave* and *Sticks and Stones* and contributor to *Brother*

To *Brother, Flesh and The Word 2, BlackOut* Magazine, *Sojourner, BGM Magazine, Out Week Magazine* and *Van Gogh's Ear.*

**FOX LEE** is an erotic fiction writer living in the Midwest. Fox has previously been published in several anthologies of gay erotica, including *Rock and Roll Over*, and *The Handsome Prince: Gay Erotic Romance* (Cleis Press). When not writing, Fox enjoys Japanese rock, Thai hip-hop, too much coffee, and Oreos.

**K. LYNN** has been a longtime fan of the erotica market, sneaking in reading time when no one was watching. She enjoys subverting gender stereotypes in her writing and looks forward to exploring that more in the future. When she's not writing short stories, she's working on her novels.

**WAYNE MANSFIELD** (waynemansfieldwrites.weebly.com) was born and raised in rural Western Australia. He has been published in collections from Lethe Press, Cleis Press and Storm Moon Press. Additionally, he has had dark erotica published by Dare Empire ("Brothers of the Moon"), Torquere Press, Damnation Books ("Tattooed") and JMS Books ("The King's Prize").

**BOB MASTERS** has had poetry published in *The James White Review* and *RFD*. He likes to write erotica in his spare time and is currently at work on his first novel.

**CHARLIE PURCELL** is living it up in China right now.

**P. L. RIPLEY** is a born storyteller weaving worlds since he could first express what he saw in his head. Fascinated with human sexuality, erotic fiction is a natural place for him to explore the connection between sexual excitement and our emotional responses to it. He lives near Bangor, Maine with his partner.

**ROB ROSEN** (www.therobrosen.com), author of the novels *Sparkle: The Queerest Book You'll Ever Love, Divas Las Vegas, Hot Lava, Southern Fried, Queerwolf,* and *Vamp,* has been published in well over 150 anthologies.

**DOMINIC SANTI** (dominicsanti@yahoo.com) is a former technical editor turned rogue whose smutty stories have appeared in dozens of anthologies, including *Wild Boys, Hot Daddies, Country Boys, Uniforms Unzipped, Beach Bums, Gay Quickies, Sexy Sailors, Middle Men* and several volumes of *Best Gay Erotica.* Plans include an even dirtier historical novel.

**K. VALE** writes erotica of all stripes. Under the name on her driver's license, she also writes horror. Stalk her on Facebook and Twitter @KimberVale or visit kimbervale.com. Come for the sex. Stay for the story.

**SALOME WILDE's** (salandtalerotica.com) diverse, pansexual erotica has appeared in collections by such editors as Susie Bright, Maxim Jakubowski and Rachel Kramer Bussel. With Talon Rihai, she is coauthor of the forthcoming M/M novella *After the First Taste of Love* (Storm Moon Press).

**LOGAN ZACHARY** (loganzacharydicklit.com) is a mystery author whose stories appear in his own collection, *Calendar Boys,* as well as in *Hard Hats, Best Gay Erotica 2009, Surfer Boys, College Boys, Skater Boys, Boys, Brief Encounters, Biker Boys, Sexy Sailors, Beach Bums* and others. His latest mystery is *Big Bad Wolf.*